Bringer of Fire

Book #1 in the Logan Bringer Series

Jaz Primo

RUTHERFORD LITERARY GROUP

www.rutherfordliterary.com

JAZ PRIMO

Published by:
Rutherford Literary Group
1205 S. Air Depot, PMB #135
Midwest City, OK 73110-4807

Cover art by Sharon Legg
Sharon Legg Digital Art

Edited by Lea Ellen Borg
Night Owl Editing Services

ISBN 0982861397
ISBN-13 978-0982861394

Novels by Jaz Primo

The Logan Bringer Urban Fantasy Series
Bringer of Fire
Bringer Unleashed *

* Additional Titles Forthcoming

∗ ∗ ∗

Gwen Reaper
(A Young Adult Paranormal Romance)
**Winner of the Paranormal Romance Guild's Reviewer's
Choice Award for Best Young Adult Novel of 2012!**

∗ ∗ ∗

The Sunset Vampire Series
Sunrise at Sunset
A Bloody London Sunset
Summit at Sunset
Wicked Sunset **
Sunset Rising **

** Additional Titles Forthcoming

∗ ∗ ∗

All titles published by Rutherford Literary Group

DEDICATION

Of the various adversities and obstacles you may face in your life, sometimes your biggest challenges are the ones found deep within you…

CONTENTS

ACKNOWLEDGMENTS

My love and thanks to my wife, Lori, for all of her continued love and support. Her thoughtful encouragement is truly inspiring. And thanks to Selina for interjecting her own special, and often amusing, insights regarding my countless hours of typing.

Once again, my heartfelt thanks to my creative and gifted cover artist, Sharon Legg, for the vivid, striking, and powerful cover art on this novel. As always, thank you to my talented and wonderful editor, Lea Ellen Borg, for her spot-on editing skills and keen eye for detail. As I continue to hone my writing craft and skills, Lea Ellen remains ever diligent in mentoring me.

Thank you to all of my friends and fans who continue to be wonderfully supportive of my literary endeavors. Though I've said this before, it bears repeating that although writing is a highly personal endeavor, it is equally rewarding to share my novels with those who experience enjoyment reading them.

i

CHAPTER 1

Brain cancer has always been an ugly disease. It's sinister. It's evil. At the age of twenty-eight, the diagnosis had shocked and horrified me into a near-fugue state. Then despair. By age twenty-nine, the cancer had nearly decimated me and the doctors soundly declared that I was terminal.

That's a hell of a thing to hear from someone.

But a last-minute opportunity to receive an experimental treatment brought a sliver of hope, and early test results were encouraging.

What followed was six long, torturous months of treatment, enduring bouts of nausea, vomiting, exhaustion, and the most debilitating sense of personal fragility of my illness thus far. If not for the strength, encouragement, and support of my friends and family, particularly my mother and sister, I doubt that I would have endured it all.

However, by the end of those challenging six months, my tumor had not only shrunk, it had practically disappeared.

During the next two months, my body slowly reconstituted itself, and I embraced cautious optimism that I might not only survive, but also hope to once again thrive. To have walked through shadows of despair and come out the other side both sane and relatively intact was one of those life-changing experiences.

To say that I was ecstatic was an understatement.

However, four days ago, my euphoria gradually changed to something altogether different. Some startling and mysterious side effects had begun to promulgate.

My curiosity gave way to concern…and then to alarm.

That's when events took a decidedly dramatic turn for the worse.

Add to that, I hated that the phone always rang at precisely the wrong time.

The shrill tone of the ringer, a sound that I kept vowing to change but never seemed to get around to, pierced through the silence of my house. The problem was I was too busy throwing up my breakfast to care.

I had been fighting a stomach virus for nearly two days.

Five minutes later as I was swishing Listerine around in my mouth, the damned phone rang again. I quickly rinsed my mouth and darted into the living room, battling a renewed queasiness in my gut.

"Hello?" I demanded.

"Logan? Are you okay?" came the anxious-sounding voice.

My sister, Lexi, mothered me even more than Mom did.

"I'm fine, Lexi. Just donating breakfast to my porcelain throne. Honestly, you'd think I was a Roman as often as I've been purging---"

"Thank God," she groaned.

"Lexi? What's wrong?"

"You're kidding. Logan, just turn on the TV," she urged. "Honestly, you're like the world's worst hermit."

I hastily searched beneath magazines, couch pillows, and a comforter for the TV remote.

"What channel?"

"Any channel!"

What had gotten into her? Had World War III started without me?

I finally found the remote underneath a rumpled pair of sweatpants. As I reached down to snatch it, the remote almost seemed to impact my palm before I actually touched it. I flinched with surprise and nearly dropped it.

"What the…"

That's precisely what had happened three days ago, except it had been a spoon that I'd reached for at breakfast.

Had I only imagined it?

"Can you see it yet?" Lexi demanded.

I hurriedly pressed the power button.

What I saw shocked me well beyond the scope of my former distractions.

"…have no idea how many people might be left inside the Wallace Building. Ambulances are streaming in as quickly as possible while fire engines rush to the scene. As you can see from the overhead vantage of Sky-6, police are rushing into the building alongside firemen to help remove victims and survivors. So far, only three people have been pulled from the blazing center alive."

The high-definition camera view from the news helicopter laid bare the full desperation of the situation. A four-story professional office complex was mostly engulfed in flames. Virtually the entire large glass facade had been blown outward, and the roof was partially collapsed at one end of the building.

"Damn," was all that I managed to say.

"Isn't that---?" Lexi asked.

Holy crap. The Wallace Building housed the Nuclegene Cancer Treatment Center.

"Yeah, that's where I've been going for my cancer treatments."

I was supposed to have been there that very day, at this very moment, in fact. But I'd contracted a stomach virus, so I had called in at the last minute to cancel.

"Oh, Logan, it's so horrible. I was afraid that you were there. I prayed so hard that you hadn't gone today, and I could barely dial the phone to call you," she managed to say through tears and sniffling.

What the hell had happened? How did an office building

just blow up like that?

The images from the circling copter were surreal. I had just been there a week ago for a cancer treatment. My mind rushed with visions of the nurses and fellow patients who I had seen and talked to then.

"I was supposed to be there today."

Suddenly, my head throbbed and my throat felt so dry that it was raw.

"I-I have to go, Sis."

I heard my sister blow her nose. "Do you want me to come over there?"

I felt numb.

"No. Just call Mom and Dad for me, will you?"

"Sure. Sure, I will," she said. "Logan, I'm just so glad that you weren't there today. After everything, I don't think I could've handled that."

I wondered who else could have made it out alive from that kind of disaster. The building was completely ablaze and smoldering debris was cast all around the area. It appeared from the various camera images that the only people being recovered were being laid underneath sheets alongside waiting ambulances.

I could've been lying beneath one of those sheets.

"Logan?"

"Yeah, I know."

I plopped down onto the couch and stared at the images before me.

"I'll call Mom and Dad and then call you back in a little while, okay? Logan?"

"Yeah, sure. Thanks, Sis," I said, staring at the televised images before me.

I put the phone down and started surfing the news channels, but the same nightmare played out before me. I couldn't move or talk, and I could barely even breathe.

Then, after a time, I managed to rise from the couch, though only to rush to the bathroom to throw up again.

* * *

Later that day, my sister brought 7Up, homemade chicken noodle soup, and saltine crackers over to me. Thankfully, Mom and Dad were still on their cruise to the Bahamas, or I'd have Mom hovering over me, as well.

Oh, I dearly loved both of them, but when I felt sick, I mostly just wanted to be left alone. Thankfully, my sister's aversion to bringing any germs back home with her that might infect her husband or my niece and nephew kept her from staying long.

My best friend, Travis Cooper, called to see if I was okay or if I needed anything. He even offered to stop by. I liked him too much to give him what I had, so I declined.

Travis and I had gone through high school together, including playing on the football team. After I served six years in the army, he had helped me get my job at the Anderson Tag Agency, where he also worked, as I completed my bachelor's degree.

Then the cancer diagnosis struck, and Travis was one of the important rocks in my life that kept me grounded through everything. Just as with my family, I owed him a lot.

Hell, whom was I fooling? Travis definitely qualified as family to me. Best of all, he knew when to give me some space when I needed it.

One thing was certain; I'd experienced enough "babysitting" during the worst of my cancer treatments. For nearly eight months, I'd moved back into my parents' house just so someone could help take care of me. I'd never felt so damned helpless in my entire life.

I'd hated the sense of helplessness even more than the friggin' cancer.

I sipped at the hot soup that Lexi had brought by.

Damn, it tasted good.

Then the reality of what had just happened washed over me again and I started to feel a little nauseous. I muted the television because the horror only continued, and the story hadn't gotten any better as evening approached.

By the time that the fire and rescue workers had started to get the fires under some sort of control, there had been only twenty-three survivors from the estimate of over two hundred and twenty occupants. I still had no idea how many of those survivors might be people I knew from the treatment center portion of the building.

Though I wasn't an avid churchgoer, I nevertheless said a number of prayers that afternoon.

I dispensed some ice cubes into a glass and poured a generous amount of 7Up into it. Mom had always given us 7Up or ginger ale when we had flu or stomach viruses as a kid. Come to think of it, I'd slurped down of a lot of both while I was sick from the cancer treatments. Not long ago, I had gratefully returned to just water, tea, and a little coffee once the new cancer drugs had started taking effect.

With the cancer at bay, I intended for my body to once again be my temple, just as it was during my time in the army.

I'd started working out again to build back the muscle mass that I'd lost. It felt great to weightlift once again. And despite the higher grocery costs, I'd even embraced both the whole and organic health foods movements. Mom and Sis were so proud of me, but my father had only laughed.

"I grew up on fried foods, and I'm doing just fine," Dad had teased.

This from a man who consumed anti-cholesterol and high blood pressure medications like vitamins.

I sipped from my glass of 7Up, only to have my memory kick back into action. My heart nearly skipped a beat.

Holy crap. My treatments.

Lost in the horror of the news reports was the realization that I had no place to go for my three remaining treatments. My momentary fear was replaced by absolute guilt as I focused on the fact that so many people had died today; people who I'd sort of grown used to seeing and commiserating with.

People who I'd grown fond of.

"I'm sitting here feeling worried about my treatments when I should feel lucky just to be alive."

Additional waves of guilt made their ugly appearance, and I went back to feeling as if I was mired in a daze. I sat on the couch sipping 7Up for the remainder of the evening.

I woke up out of a deep sleep with a start. The television was on, and I checked the time on the DVR. It was around 3 a.m.

But something was wrong.

At least, something felt different.

My mind felt completely clear, devoid of the bout of anxiety and depression that I'd felt earlier. Instead, I felt at peace.

"Strange," I muttered.

I got up to stretch and felt only a slight degree of weakness in the pit of my stomach. Maybe the virus was finally working its way out of my system.

But I still felt a little icky and wandered into the bathroom to take a shower.

The hot water was soothing and I felt better than I had in days. While I was still somber about what had happened the previous day, I detected an absurd sense of calmness inside of me.

I hated to admit that it felt good.

After washing my hair, I reached out for the soap.

It slapped into the palm of my hand like it had been thrown there!

My eyes darted to and fro, half-expecting someone to be standing there after having handed me the soap. I looked at the soap dish. It was nearly a foot away from me.

"No way."

What the hell was going on?

There was nobody I could call. The office building that served as the only contact for my treatments was destroyed, and for all I knew, everybody who had worked there might be dead.

So much for a calming sense of peace.

After I got out of the shower, I looked in the mirror at the visage of a guy who was way too young to look that tired and out of sorts. I ran my fingers across the faint scar running across my chin where an enemy bullet had grazed it during my tour of duty in Afghanistan during the nation's second invasion of that country following the collapse of the country's formerly sectarian government.

Yet another occasion when Lady Luck had been watching over me.

I ran my fingers through my once-again healthy head of hair, grateful that it'd finally grown out again. Fortunately, the experimental treatments hadn't caused hair loss like my previous bouts of chemotherapy and radiation had.

My mind gravitated back to the soap episode in the shower.

Had I been hallucinating?

In the absence of an explanation, I did the only thing that I thought any clueless person might do under similar circumstances—I started Googling for answers.

Hours later, I gave up on Google. It had been of little or no help. That is, unless I wanted to believe that I was spontaneously becoming a Jedi Knight.

I could almost believe there really was a test to measure something called midi-chlorians.

Geeks and nerds were so creative.

Likewise, I didn't think that any of *The X-Files* episodes that had been referenced were applicable.

I'd never been part of the nerdy crowd, but I had to admit that, years ago, I'd appreciated watching *The X-Files*. It'd seemed much more grounded than typical science fiction.

Whatever happened to Gillian Anderson, anyway?

She was so hot.

During my Internet searching, I'd read some information on telekinesis, the ability to move objects with one's mind. However, I wasn't certain that I hadn't been hallucinating versus actually moving inanimate objects.

Still, I *had* held the soap in my hand. Hallucinations

didn't usually generate lather.

In the end, I had no more prospective answers than when I'd started, and I still had no idea about what to do next.

I glanced at the clock and realized that it was almost eight in the morning. It was Tuesday, and I'd normally be expected into work at the tag agency by nine. While I'd taken Monday off due to illness, my boss had always been kind enough to give me my cancer treatment days off, as well.

However, I still felt a little puny from having the stomach flu, so I reached for the phone to call in sick.

The phone unexpectedly propelled into my hand like someone had tossed it to me!

I sat there feeling stunned as I stared at the phone like it was an alien artifact.

"I damned sure didn't hallucinate that," I said aloud, if only to reassure myself that I was still grounded in reality.

Then a haunting thought occurred to me.

Do insane people realize that they're hallucinating?

A couple of seconds later, the phone rang and I abruptly dropped it, as if it had burned my hand or something. It rang two more times before I built up the nerve to snatch it up to answer it.

"Yeah?" I asked gruffly.

"Mr. Bringer?"

The woman's tentative voice sounded familiar to me.

"Yes, this is Logan Bringer."

"This is Maria Edwards from the treatment center."

I knew her. Maria was the cute physician's assistant who periodically met with me during my treatments.

A hopeful feeling surged through me as I realized that at least one person I knew had survived yesterday's disaster.

"Maria! My God, are you okay?"

I heard what sounded like a sigh of relief.

"Mr. Bringer, I'm fine, thanks. I can't really say much right now. The police asked me to contact as many staff and patients associated with our office as I could and then report back to them."

"Who else---"

"You're the first person that I managed to---"

Then I heard her start crying.

"Listen, Maria, I'm so sorry about your co-workers. I-I just don't know what to say. I thought that I was the only person left for all I knew."

I waited as she blew her nose and pulled herself together enough to speak again.

"I'm sorry. It's just so overwhelming, Mr.---"

"No, call me Logan."

She blew her nose again.

"Okay. But I really have to keep calling. There's still half the list left."

"Yeah, I understand."

This entire situation was just so unreal.

"Listen, Maria, what do I do? I mean, should I---"

"No. The police said that they will meet with anyone who's associated in any way with the building. The only thing that I can suggest is that you just stay near your phone for now."

That didn't sound particularly hopeful.

"Okay, thanks, Maria. Listen, are you going to be okay for now?"

"Yeah. Thanks, Logan. I need to do this."

"Take care of yourself, okay?"

"Sure, I'll try. You too."

After I hung up the phone, I dialed the tag agency to call in sick for the day. Then I turned on the news.

The reporters were all speculating on a host of possible causes for the office building disaster, including an act of terrorism.

But if it's terrorism, who would want to blow up an ordinary office building?

CHAPTER 2

I spent the remainder of the day and that evening half resting at home and half wondering if I was going insane. I called my sister to touch base, but Mom still called to check on me just before dinnertime. Travis called again, as well.

I almost told Travis about my strange side effects—or hallucinations?—but thought better of it for the time being. He'd probably think that I was crazy.

But then, maybe I was.

Perhaps that was why I didn't dare try to tell either Lexi or my mother; I was hesitant over how they might react, too.

I ate more soup and crackers and drank more 7Up.

Damn, I'd almost forgotten how good cola tasted, and despite my health food mantra, I vowed that it would maintain its presence in my future diet.

Maybe it was merely the sugar, but my mood had quickly improved and my mind felt somewhat more settled. If only my stomach would return to normal as quickly.

The next day, I actually made it into work. It felt almost strange to be there, but at least it brought me back into more of a normal routine. Each of my coworkers asked how I was feeling and my boss, Larry Anderson, was also really supportive, but everyone acted somewhat tentative toward me, except for Travis.

"Hey, Dracula, shouldn't you be back at home in your crypt?" he teased.

I sneered. "Thanks, buddy, you're all heart."

"Hey, I'm just sayin' you look a little pale, that's all."

"Yeah, well, stomach flu tends to do that to a person."

His facial expression turned serious.

"Listen, Logan, we were all glued to the TV in the break room yesterday. I'm still pretty shocked about the explosion. You okay?"

I sighed.

Good question. Am I okay?

"As okay as anybody gets under the circumstances, I suppose."

"I keep thinking about what might have happened if you'd gone to your treatment yesterday," he said.

I looked at him and noted the serious expression on his face.

"Yeah, me too."

Within a couple of hours, I'd fallen into a pleasant workday rhythm and life began to feel a little more like normal. For a while, it felt good to distract myself with the mundane world of driver's licenses and vehicle registrations. But eventually, I thought back to my conversation with Maria, and I felt morose all over again.

Honestly, I felt like a bit of a wreck emotionally.

Still, I made it through the day without losing either my mind or my lunch. By the time I made it home that evening, I felt physically exhausted. I made a light supper of more soup and crackers with a mug of hot tea, which made me chuckle.

I would receive such a world of shit from my army buddies if they saw me sitting here savoring a mug of hot tea.

But then a lot had changed since those days.

I'd given a lot of thought to what I had experienced with the soap in the shower and later with the telephone, and arrived at a decision: *In the absence of normal logic, explore the outlandish.*

After I finished eating, I cleared the small dining room

table of everything except the salt and pepper shakers, a pencil, and an ink pen. I placed everything in the center of the table so the items weren't touching one another.

Then I sat down in one of the chairs and stared at each item while concentrating on making one of them move. If I could inadvertently cause soap bars, telephone handsets, and TV remotes to leap into my hand, perhaps I could deliberately manipulate one of the items before me.

However, after nearly an hour, during which time I felt like some hack magician, all that I managed to do was hold my breath and coax a vein to pop out on my forehead. It really pissed me off.

What was I missing?

I placed my palm face up on the table and concentrated on making the pencil or ink pen go to my hand.

Nothing.

"Figures." I held my hand palm outward to each of the writing utensils and imagined one of them leaping into my palm.

No response.

I tried for another twenty minutes.

Nothing.

I slammed my palm onto the tabletop in aggravation. The pen and pencil both rolled around a little bit.

"Yeah, that's successful. It's called the magic of vibration."

The entire evening had given me a pounding headache, so I got up to take a couple of Tylenol capsules with some 7Up.

Minutes later, and to my surprise, I could feel my head beginning to clear.

"Damn, if that Tylenol isn't great stuff."

I wandered over to the TV remote control and tuned into the news. I'd become used to checking for periodic updates on the explosion.

Placing the remote control atop the coffee table, or rather on top of all the junk stacked on it, I turned to look back at the items on the dining room table. I held out my hand and concentrated on bringing any one of the items to me.

Nothing.

"What a load of crap! I must've been hallucinating after all."

However, rather than reassuring me, that only scared me. What if I'm losing my marbles after everything I've been through?

It succeeded in making me feel angry.

I pointed an accusing finger at the items on the dining room table, wishing that I could cast them across the room.

"Move, damn you!"

A sudden series of loud knocks against the front door startled me, and the pencil, paper, and salt and pepper shakers flew off the table, impacting the far wall as if they had been thrown.

I stared across the room in awe.

"No way."

The knocking on the front door startled me back to reality again.

I was torn between rushing to the dining room to pick up the items and going to answer the door, but propriety won, and I headed to the door.

I was greeted by a man and a woman, each wearing dark suits.

"Mr. Logan Bringer?" asked the man.

"Yes."

Both of them flipped open black leather wallets that revealed badges and ID cards.

"We're with the FBI. I'm Special Agent Ted Burroughs, and this is Special Agent Megan Sanders. We'd like to visit with you if you have a few minutes to spare."

I was somewhat surprised. I'd expected to be contacted by the local police, but not the FBI.

But there they stood in my doorway. It was the sort of thing that I had only seen on television. Maybe like on... *The*

X-Files.

"Sounds reasonable," I said.

The lady agent—did he say her name was Sanders?—looked at me with a curious expression.

"May we come in?" she asked.

"Yeah, sure," I replied and held the door open for them to enter.

It was then that I cast a disparaging look at the state of my living room. After closing the door, I awkwardly cleared off the pillows, comforter, and laundry from the couch and piled them on the floor at one end of the couch.

"Please, have a seat."

Agent Burroughs looked like the poster child for FBI agents with his closely cropped haircut, athletic build, and neatly pressed suit. He appeared to be sizing me up, as well, and part of me got the impression that he was resisting the urge to shake his head.

Meanwhile, Agent Sanders also seemed to be assessing me, though with a bit more amusement. Her hazel eyes seemed to twinkle slightly and she appeared to be trying to suppress her amusement.

"You'll have to pardon the mess," I said.

"Not a problem," Sanders offered. "We don't assess you on your housekeeping."

However, Agent Burroughs appeared to be intently focused on the items lying across the room on the floor, not far from the dining room table.

I bet that guy catches everything.

"Can I get either of you something to drink? I have juice and bottled water," I said. "Oh, and 7Up."

They both declined, so I perched on the edge of the reading chair that was relatively devoid of laundry.

I really should try to clean this place up.

Not that I'd expected to entertain the FBI anytime soon. And it wasn't like I'd been having dinner parties, either. I'd discovered that not knowing if you're going to be among the living in the near future or not tended to put a damper on one's social activities.

"No, nothing for us, thanks," Agent Sanders replied.

I couldn't help thinking that she had striking eyes, and I liked the way that her short, auburn hair framed her features. Of course, the fact that such things came to my attention punctuated the fact that I hadn't been on a date in a long time, either.

"What can I do for you this evening?" I asked.

"Mr. Bringer, we're investigating the expl---" Sanders began.

"Mr. Bringer, can you tell me your whereabouts this past Monday evening and until Tuesday morning?" Agent Burroughs abruptly cut her off.

To her credit, Agent Sanders glared daggers at him.

Despite my unexpected circumstances, I'd been carefully observing my visitors in much the same manner that they appeared to be assessing me.

I determined that while they were close to my age, Burroughs was definitely the senior. For that reason and more, I also estimated that Sanders was not only the junior partner, but none too pleased about that fact, either.

"Here at home. I was ill with a stomach virus," I smoothly replied.

Burroughs scribbled on a notepad that he had extracted from his jacket pocket. It appeared in his hand like such a classic FBI prop that I almost laughed aloud. I remembered when my Dad used to watch old *Dragnet* episodes on TV when I was growing up.

"Can you name any witnesses who can corroborate that?"

So the guy was going all "Joe Friday" from *Dragnet* on me, after all.

Just the facts.

"I took part in a number of phone calls during that time, and my sister came over Tuesday morning after she called to tell me about the building explosion."

I had no illusions as to why the FBI was visiting me.

Hell, I was a patient in that building, after all.

"Is it correct that you were receiving treatments at the Nuclegene cancer treatment center in the Wallace Building?"

"Yes."

"What type of cancer were you being treated for?" Sanders asked.

"Terminal brain cancer."

I added terminal for dramatic effect. Sanders' expression softened but Burroughs seemed unimpressed.

"When did you last visit the Wallace Building?" Burroughs asked.

"A week ago Tuesday."

"When were you due to go there again?" Sanders asked.

"Tuesday morning of this week."

Sanders stared at me and her lips parted slightly with the undeniable recognition that I had dodged one of fate's biggest bullets.

"Why didn't you go to the Wallace Building on Tuesday morning as scheduled?" Burroughs pressed.

I stared back at him.

"Because I had a stomach virus."

Somebody's not paying attention.

"Mr. Burroughs, your army personnel file indicates that one of your specialties was in demolitions. Is that correct?"

I quickly realized where the direction the conversation was headed.

"Yes."

"Describe that in more detail for us," he said.

"I was on a fire team during two tours in Afghanistan and one of my specialties was in demolitions. I helped to render useless a variety of weapons caches, as well as fight Islamic insurgents."

"Only two? A lot of soldiers have served more than just two tours overseas," Burroughs said.

I frowned, unsure where he was going with that.

"I served six years, and then returned to civilian life only to discover that I had brain cancer."

"Tough break," Burroughs said, though without any convincing sense of sympathy. "I'm sure that you felt a little resentful about that."

"It's worth pointing out that Nuclegene center was the key solution standing between me and oblivion. I had three more treatments left to take, not to mention that some of my fellow patients grew to feel like friends of mine, so one might imagine that I wasn't happy to see the building go up in flames with them in it."

"Mm-hm," he murmured.

It's said that first impressions are everything. Agent Burroughs seemed to be a bit of an asshole.

"Mr. Bringer, do you have any idea who would want to destroy the Wallace Building or kill any of its occupants?" Sanders asked.

"No idea at all," I said.

What a waste of so many innocent lives.

What's more, none of the other offices seemed like a typical target for terrorists in my opinion. Why would someone want to blow up the building in the first place?

It didn't make sense.

Sanders started to ask something but Burroughs cut her off.

"Where are you currently employed, or perhaps I should ask, are you currently employed?"

My first impression that the guy seemed like an asshole was confirmed. So, now he's asking if I might be a freeloader or drain on society, too?

My former army discipline kicked in at just the right time and I politely answered his questions. He continued with additional questions about my family, friends, and co-workers. There were also additional queries into my background that were either relatively public knowledge or fully covered in my army personnel records.

I looked at Agent Sanders, who had remained quiet throughout the interview, occasionally nodding and scribbling on her own notepad or observing me with a thoughtful expression.

"Mr. Bringer, I recommend that you don't leave town anytime soon. We may want to interview you further," Burroughs announced.

He stood and Sanders followed his lead. They walked to the front door to leave, but Sanders turned at the last moment and handed me a business card.

"My contact information is on that card if you remember anything that you'd like to add or think of something further that might be helpful in our investigation."

I took the card and looked at her. At least she'd been polite. Meanwhile, Burroughs was already halfway back to their car.

I watched Sanders hurry to catch up with her partner, and I couldn't help but notice that even in her formal slacks she had a cute butt.

"God, I really need to start dating again."

I glanced down at the business card that Agent Sanders had handed me.

Special Agent Megan Sanders, Counterterrorism Investigations.

I normally tossed business cards onto the mail pile on my coffee table. However, this time I actually programmed Agent Sanders' information into my cell phone. Given the gravity of the situation and Burroughs questions, I had the uneasy feeling that I might be seeing more of both agents in the not-too-distant future.

CHAPTER 3

I sat on the living room couch for what seemed like forever after the agents left my home. It was important for me to consider all of the angles related to both my physical and mental condition and the pending investigations that I had been drawn into. The worst thing that I could do would be to continue in the chaotic manner that I had been.

Granted, I'd done nothing wrong. But I had the distinct impression that I had already become more than a passing person of interest in the eyes of the authorities.

Should I secure an attorney? Maybe I should ask my Dad for advice?

While both were excellent choices, I settled on a more immediate concern; namely, my sanity, or possible lack thereof.

I picked up the phone—devoid of weird Jedi-like affects this time—and cycled through the caller ID until I found Maria Edwards, the physician's assistant from the treatment center who had called me.

The phone rang only twice before she picked up.

"Hello?"

"Maria, this is Logan Bringer. I really need to talk to you."

Silence.

"Um, okay," she said hesitantly.

Her voice sounded strange. Had the FBI been to see her already?

"Maria, I know this is going to come off as kind of weird, but I've noticed some odd side effects during the past week, and I wondered if it might be from the treatments that I've been taking."

Silence.

"Maria?"

"Yes, I'm still here. What sort of side effects?"

I swallowed hard, wondering if I was about to admit something that would end with me being admitted into a mental facility.

Given everything, I was fairly certain that the FBI would probably love that. Or, at least, Agent Burroughs might.

"Well, Maria, I've had a couple of instances where objects kind of---"

I stopped to collect my thoughts.

"What I mean is, on occasion, I might be misjudging my perception of objects and their relative distance from me."

Okay, that sounded all wrong.

"I-I'm not sure what you mean," she stammered.

"Maria, I think that objects are sometimes either attracted or repelled by me."

Yep, that sounded completely mental. Way to go, Logan.

I expected Maria to laugh or perhaps hang up, but instead I thought that I heard a sharp intake of breath.

"Logan, I want you to come to my house. There's something that you need to know."

I was surprised.

"Really? Tonight?"

"Tonight, Logan. Right now, in fact. And I'd rather not discuss this over the phone. Here's my address…"

I scribbled her address on the cover of a sports magazine that was lying on my coffee table and assured her that I was on my way. I was intrigued by her reaction and so curious what she might say that not even the entire FBI could stop me from getting to her house that night.

Half an hour later, I pulled into the driveway of the address that she had given me. Maria lived in a relatively new neighborhood across town from me.

Even at night, the hedges and lawn looked immaculate. I felt so anxious to speak to her that I practically hopped from the car and onto her front porch. She must've been watching for me because my finger never had a chance to touch the doorbell.

"Come in, Logan. I'm glad that you called me tonight," Maria said as she held open her front door for me.

The interior of her home looked both elegant and immaculate, making me feel as though I lived in a dump by comparison. She looked quite attractive in her faded blue jeans and dark pullover sweater as she gestured for me to sit on her couch.

She perched nervously on the edge of the couch cushion next to me and tried unsuccessfully to appear reassuring.

"Would you like something to drink? Maybe tea or coffee?" she asked.

Something to drink? The great American greeting. My thoughts shot back to my earlier meeting with the FBI.

"No, thanks, I'm fine," I replied.

Actually, I'm *not* fine.

"Logan, these symptoms that you described to me over the phone, are you certain they had something to do with the unexpected moving of objects?" she asked.

I nodded.

"What I'm about to tell you is—well, rather incredible, but also potentially dangerous."

Part of me wasn't sure if I wanted to know what she was going to say next.

"Go on," I said. "Whatever it is, I need to know. I think I'm going crazy or something."

She offered me a sympathetic expression.

"Logan, you're not going crazy. The things you're experiencing are side effects of your treatment. Other patients have experienced them before. It's just that you're---"

"What? I'm what?"

I was really somewhat anxious at that point. The army never trained me on how to react to shit like this.

"You're one of the few patients who has made it this far before. Most didn't survive their treatments."

Both my mind and pulse raced. Of all the things she could have told me, that definitely wasn't something I expected.

"All of the patients in your program are—well, were— terminal cancer patients just like you," she explained as she reached out to take one of my hands in hers. "The drug has demonstrated an amazing effect on cancer tumors, but much of the time a patient's cancer overtakes the pace of the treatment. You see, using terminal patients is the only way that the government will allow us to conduct trial testing of the drug."

"But recent tests have shown my tumor is shrinking," I said.

She smiled genuinely then.

"Yes, you're one of the lucky ones. In fact, I've already seen your latest results from the brain scan that you took nearly two weeks ago, and your tumor has gone from small to undetectable. You were supposed to find out on Tuesday, but then---" she stopped abruptly.

"Yeah, that."

We both fell silent.

"Logan, there's something else you should know."

I looked into her green eyes and easily read the apprehension in them.

"I've been a PA in this experimental program almost since the start of it over three years ago," she said. "But recently, I was curious about what the success rate has been for patients undergoing the treatments. About three weeks ago, I used a workstation that one of our team doctors had left himself logged into and read the results being recorded in the centralized patient database."

She paused and took a deep breath.

"Please promise not to tell anyone else that I'm telling you this because I could get fired. Who knows, maybe even worse."

I frowned. Just what kind of company was she working for?

"Then why are you telling me?" I asked.

She let go of my hand abruptly.

"Because they shouldn't be withholding this information from you; it's simply not ethical. You're one of the few patients in the program who were fortunate enough to survive to this stage. I found out that the patients are only being given the drug to affect their tumors so that the FDA will permit the use of terminal human subjects," she said. "Nuclegene's primary research was never about curing tumors. That's just a beneficial secondary use for the drug; something acting as a catalyst in the serum also attacks most cancer tissues. Their real interest is about what happens to people if they survived the treatment on their tumors. Some patients like yourself have beaten their cancers only to die from complications of the drug. However, the causes of deaths were conveniently recorded as complications from their cancers. The company was using the cancers merely to mask their true research."

I was definitely shocked. What she just told me sounded like the plot from a sci-fi film.

Once again, *THE X-Files* came to mind.

Great, now I'm OCD.

I momentarily rubbed at my temples with my fingertips.

Stay focused, Logan.

"What's the actual purpose of the drug?" I asked.

"Nuclegene is attempting to stimulate and manifest development of parts of the human brain that generally go unused. Logan, according to the information that I read, they're trying to manifest psychic abilities, including telekinesis."

Moving objects.

I'd actually been causing the objects to move.

"Okay. Maybe I'm not insane, but that's just plain crazy."

She arched her eyebrows at me.

"Weren't you the one who was just telling me that objects were moving on their own?"

Despite the seriousness of the conversation, the corners of my mouth upturned slightly. The lighter moment lasted long enough for me to recount something she'd revealed moments ago.

"You said that other patients died even after beating their cancers. How did they die?"

Maria's expression turned somber.

"Mostly from strokes, brain aneurisms, and in one case, suicide. Her name was Betsy, and according to the records, she developed melancholia and then severe clinical depression."

I groaned. "You're just full of good news, aren't you, lady?"

She gently grasped my arm.

"Listen, you're the youngest survivor to reach this stage. There's no reason to believe that you can't beat the odds. I found out that most patients were well over 40. You're only in your late twenties, and frankly, in far better physical condition than any of our usual patients."

She fell silent again.

"I can't help thinking about all my co-workers and patients," she whispered hoarsely before starting to cry.

I reached over to her coffee table to retrieve a few tissues from a Kleenex box and handed them to her.

As she dabbed at her nose, I put my arm around her and pulled her to me in a supportive embrace.

"Thanks for telling me all this, Maria. And I promise not to get you in trouble."

Maria snuffled into her tissues while I contemplated all that she'd said.

"I just have one question."

She blew her nose. "What's that?"

"What the hell am I supposed to do with these revelations?"

"I don't know, Logan," she conceded. "I already reported to the company's central office on the survivors listing, so they may be contacting you soon."

"Other survivors? Who else survived?" I asked.

"Just you, me, and a data entry clerk. But we were all out of the office that day. Nobody from our office who was inside the building that day actually survived."

My God. How horrible.

"Logan, there's something else about the company. From the test results I saw, your cancer is probably cured. But the scan images were already posted in the company's central database, so eventually they'll see the results, as well. There are regions of your brain that are lit up like a Christmas tree. Based on that alone, they're probably going to want to do more tests on you."

I didn't want to end up as a human guinea pig.

"I could always refuse. Better yet, let them test me. It doesn't really matter. I can't control what I'm doing anyway. Half the time, I just get a headache if I try, and nothing comes of it unless I'm upset."

I recalled the items from my dining room table from earlier that evening.

"Even then, the results are erratic and more often than not result in a mess," I added.

Maria pulled away from me slightly and pressed a small USB memory stick into my palm.

"What this?" I asked.

"It's a copy of the test results that I just mentioned. I started making copies of materials soon after I gained access to patient records."

"Isn't that kind of dangerous?"

She nodded. "Yeah, but I didn't have time to review everything that I discovered online, so my curiosity got the better of me. I'd planned to erase the data once I was finished, but the explosion got me thinking---" she stopped abruptly.

"About?"

"Wild thoughts," she whispered.

I let my mind wonder at that. I was beginning to have wild thoughts, as well.

"There's something else. Electrolytes," she said.

"What?"

"The company's notes made a lot of references to electrolytes."

I thought about that for a moment.

"Like the stuff your body burns when you exercise?"

That was something they always preached to us in the military after hard workouts and prolonged marches.

Replenish your electrolytes.

"Exactly. And where do you replenish electrolytes from?" she asked.

"Gatorade?"

"Or most any soda," she added.

"Like 7Up," I breathed with sudden realization.

She nodded.

Then something else occurred to me.

"Maria, what happens if I don't receive the last three treatments that I was scheduled for?"

She frowned.

"I really don't recommend taking any more of that drug, Logan. With your tumor gone, for all we know, additional applications of the drug might not only be unnecessary, but also lethal," she warned.

Lethal.

It felt like I'd been sparring with lethal for most of my adult life, just in different settings or involving other circumstances.

"What are you going to do now?" she asked.

"You mean, aside from trying to convince the FBI that I'm not a terrorist?" I quipped. "Actually, I need to go to the grocery store."

She stared back at me with a blank expression.

* * *

I had no further contact with Maria after we met at her house that evening. By Friday, I was relieved that any lingering weakness due to my stomach virus had thankfully dissipated. Better yet, there'd been no further visits from the FBI.

Perhaps best of all, I felt some peace of mind that my brain cancer might actually have been cured. However, for the time being, I kept the news regarding my latest brain scan results to myself. I was so eager to tell my parents and sister the great news, as well as my friends, but something told me that discretion was the better part of valor for the time being.

Maria's revelations regarding the Nuclegene Corporation hadn't settled well with me. Somehow, the company that I had mentally associated with giving me a second chance at life suddenly seemed less beneficent and much more nefarious. Yet, nobody else from the company had tried to contact me yet, either.

My mind was in constant motion as I contemplated the various angles of what I'd experienced, coupled with what I'd learned from Maria. My only attempt to read the information from the USB memory drive that Maria had given to me had resulted in very little helpful information. Most of the data was heavily laden with medical and technical jargon that left me bewildered.

Instead, I secured the drive in a relatively hidden location. It might have merely been paranoia on my part, but it seemed the sensible thing to do.

Friday evening after work, Travis came over to share a pizza while we watched a rerun of *The Expendables 2* with Sylvester Stallone and a host of other old action hero stars.

Despite partaking in an unhealthy pizza, I let Travis consume the beers that he'd brought while I guzzled Gatorade; something that I'd been doing since Wednesday evening.

My headaches had virtually stopped, but I had yet to successfully move objects selectively. Instead, objects erratically moved either to me or away from me from time to time.

Earlier that day at the tag agency, a stapler I'd reached for leapt into my hand at the last moment just before I touched it. Fortunately, nobody had noticed.

However, I resolved that over the weekend I needed to make a breakthrough of some kind because I couldn't continue to risk unpredictable events that might draw undue attention to me.

One thing was certain; if strange abilities were being manifested within me, I wanted to control them rather than wait for some corporate lab to take the reins. I hated the idea of becoming someone else's lab rat!

Of course, I had no illusions about ever making use of my odd abilities. Quite honestly, the effects were so subtle that they seemed more annoying than useful.

My goal was to return to a relatively normal and cancer-free life. To me, that was success.

I felt hopeful; at least, until Saturday night.

I had visited my sister and her family during the day, and spent time outside tossing the football around with my nephew, Jake, and brother-in-law, Kevin. Following that, my parents arrived, and we held a family barbeque. Mom and Dad told us about their recent Caribbean cruise and showed us way too many photos from their exploits. It was enjoyable until early evening when I suddenly broke out in a cold sweat and my headache returned with a vengeance.

I told everyone that I was just feeling a little tired from a long day and needed to go home to rest, but my sister gave me a look as if she knew better. I came directly home and collapsed onto my couch. Despite drinking what felt like a gallon of Gatorade, I still felt weak and eventually fell asleep.

I had surreal, vivid dreams about electricity coursing along the ground, and then a series of lightning storms that erupted in the sky. Then there were black, roaring tornadoes in my dream, and all manner of things were flying through the air such as houses, vehicles, trees limbs, and various other objects.

Abruptly, I woke from my dream with a gasp. My lungs were heaving and my head pounded like hammers were beating on my brain.

The room was dark but there was the sound of thunder and flashes of lightning through the living room window. My body felt drenched with sweat and my clothes stuck to my skin.

Lightning flashed again, and I was shocked by what I saw. My living room looked like it had been trashed!

The coffee table was tipped over, the reading chair had been pushed into the dining room, and the lamp from the end table lie upon the floor. Clothes, magazines, and other personal effects were chaotically strewn around the room.

What the hell had happened?

I felt disoriented, anxious, and thirsty all at the same time. I managed to reach down onto the floor where my Gatorade bottle had fallen. I twisted off the cap and drank the remaining contents even as I tried to grasp what had occurred.

My mind quickly began to clear and I rolled off of the couch and staggered into the dining room to flip on the light switch. Fortunately, the chaos appeared to be contained to my living room.

I went to the refrigerator to extract a bottle of 7Up, which I downed in a matter of seconds.

My mind raced from feeling dazed to feeling practically energized.

Oh, I felt amazing!

My body felt alive; nearly electric and hypersensitive.

On a whim, I held out my hand to the dining room table and looked at the salt shaker.

Nothing happened, but my hand tingled slightly.

Then I tried again, except this time I imagined the shaker coming to me. A pressure formed against my palm, as if something was already touching my skin.

To my shock, the shaker smacked into my palm like it had been thrown at me!

"Well I'll be Sierra Hotel," I muttered.

I was stunned.

Thunder roared outside and lighting flashed through the curtains like a pronouncement from Mount Olympus.

Despite my vivid, strange dreams, something significant had changed in my body while I'd slept.

Something fantastic!

A barrier had suddenly been breached; hurdling past frustration and futility and landing firmly into a space reserved for things phenomenally unknown.

I realized that my life was about to become even more interesting.

Unfortunately, experience had taught me that the most dangerous aspect about eye-opening revelations wasn't when I was mistaken, but rather when I was correct.

CHAPTER 4

I spent Sunday at home relentlessly practicing moving objects. It felt as if some invisible gateway had been partially opened the previous night, permitting me access to something formerly unassailable.

I was like a kid with a new toy.

By the end of the day, I'd learned that extended periods of moving even small objects like pencils, articles of clothing, and magazines generated headaches, as well as caused me to break out in a sweat.

The largest object I managed to move was a dining room chair, though barely more than a foot or so before my head was once again pounding.

Fortunately, it seemed that Maria had been correct about electrolytes. Colas and sports drinks kept the headaches in check and helped me to concentrate, acting almost like fuel for my abilities.

Despite plying my body with all manner of energy drinks, I felt exhausted by the end of the day. However, I felt more alive than I had in a long time.

That night I slept like the proverbial dead.

By Monday morning, I could hardly concentrate on my work. There were so many wayward questions running though my brain, and I craved solid answers.

During my mid-morning break, I called Maria on my cell phone and quickly explained the recent developments in my newfound abilities. Despite her former misgivings, she seemed greatly interested.

"Maria, there's something I really need to know. When you looked at my most recent brain scan, was there any comparison data?" I asked. "I'd like to know how my results compared to the scans of other patients who received the same treatments."

"From what I recall, overall your brain appeared to be much more active than the majority of the other patients. However, there were small regions of your bran that weren't as brightly lit as a few of the others. I can't be certain, but that might be due to tissue variances where your tumor was located. There's a possibility that additional applications of the drug may improve the results in those regions, but I don't recommend further treatments. Don't forget what I said happened to most of the other patients."

"Yeah, I remember. It really doesn't matter, I suppose, what with the explosion and everything."

I probably should've just stopped there and let things drop, but I'd made a lot of progress over the weekend.

I almost laughed.

Hell, it wasn't as if I had any practical use for the abilities; not many job opportunities out there for telekinetic freaks, short of circus sideshows.

"Logan," Maria prompted.

"Yeah?"

"Never mind. Forget it."

"What? What were you thinking?" I asked.

The line went silent for a moment.

"You're thinking about the drug, aren't you?"

"Yeah, I suppose I am."

She sighed.

"Listen, the reason I wasn't in the office on the day of the explosion was because I had gone across town to pick up a fresh delivery of the drug for the treatment center. It's still in my refrigerator, in fact. But I've already told the company and they're supposed to be by sometime this afternoon to pick it up," she said.

She had some of the drug in her refrigerator?

Her revelation intrigued me.

Maybe if I took just one more dose?

Granted, I didn't want to end up like those poor folks who'd succumbed to strokes over it.

"Do you think that another treatment would significantly enhance anything?" I asked.

Maria sighed.

"Possibly, but there's no way to know for certain."

"Unless I tried," I said.

"It'd have to be today, Logan. Right now, in fact. For all I know, they may already be on their way here to get the shipment."

My heart raced over the possibilities, or more accurately, the gamble.

Why risk it? What's to be gained?

A smart man would've been thankful just to have the possibility for a full, cancer-free life. What were the practical benefits for me even if I were able to enhance my abilities?

"Logan?"

"Yeah, I hear you. I'm probably not even thinking clearly right---"

"If you want to try just one dose, I'll administer it to you. But you'd have to come over *now*."

I felt as if I was at a crossroads in my life; like the ultimate game show moment where I might risk losing everything. I could almost hear the game show host say, *"Take what you have now, or risk it all for what's behind curtain number two. Winner takes all."*

I was probably being foolhardy, but I'd always heard that he who hesitates is lost.

Yet, he who leaps without looking might also be lost.

Nothing ventured, nothing gained?

Crap.

"I'll be right over."

* * *

I sat on Maria's couch blankly staring at her television as she retrieved the medication intended for me. A voice in the back of my mind nagged at me, telling me it was idiotic to take another treatment.

I couldn't help feeling that maybe that voice was right. My problem was that I was too damned curious to say no.

What could I say? Stubbornness had always been a predominant trait in me.

"Earlier today, Utah Republican Senator Benjamin Conway spoke out regarding the recent explosion at the Wallace Building, named after multi-billionaire American investor, Nevis Wallace, long-known to be one of Conway's key campaign contributors," said a television reporter.

I concentrated on the screen before me.

"This cowardly act of terrorism will not go unpunished," Senator Conway said. "We're a proud nation of patriots, and we'll never permit the evils in the world to go unchallenged, particularly when perpetrated on American soil."

I'd never cared much for Benjamin Conway; one of the Senate's most outspoken members. Frankly, I'd always considered him to be a bit of a pompous ass. Granted, I didn't entirely disagree with that he'd just said, but he'd always come off as overly zealous when it came to topics like terrorism.

I recalled how Conway had made the topic of terrorism his personal centerpiece and agenda for the nation, pushing through a number of legislative bills to increase the strengths, and reach, of law enforcement.

He'd called it his crusade, of sorts. Personally, I've never been a fan of paranoid tendencies when it came to my government. But then, that's just me.

"...regarding the demonstrations that are taking place nearly ten years following the historic Land Reclamation and

Investment in America Act. Many Americans believe that it was wrong to declare imminent domain on large stretches of individually-owned farmland and grassland in key areas across America, enabling the largest corporations to construct cities that catered to their own designs," said the news anchor.

"While intended to create potentially millions of new jobs and spur the economic growth of the United States, the act worried many civil liberties and privacy advocates. Today, we asked Senator Conway about that. Many remember that Conway, who was a key member of the Republican supermajority in control, in conjunction with a Republican-controlled White House, had helped push through the controversial legislation nearly a decade ago," continued the news anchor.

I stared at the television, taking in the Senator's beaming smile. He looked like an overly sly investment broker who'd just bilked some old lady out of her retirement savings.

"The Land Reclamation and Investment in America Act continues to propel the United States back to being the world's premiere economic superpower," he said. "Millions of jobs are still being created in vital areas of construction, supply, and service industries across this great nation of ours. Throughout history, business and industry was central to America's growth and success. And now, it's shaping America into something even greater; something that our children's children will continue to reap the benefits of."

I wasn't sure that I agreed with the senator. However, one thing seemed certain in my mind; our nation had changed considerably during my lifetime.

It wasn't the era of big government; nor was it the era of small government. It was the undeniable era of corporations.

"But Senator, what of the thousands of Americans who live in many major cities that have been abandoned by these same corporations who are relocating to the new corporate-owned cities, leaving a trail of urban blight and decay in their path?"

The Senator's features turned serious.

"During every major industrial and economic period of rebirth in our nation's history, there've always been winners and losers. Yet, I'm comfortable knowing that there will be more winners than losers. Besides, nothing stays the same forever. Boom towns rise and fall, but our nation has always bounced back stronger than before from the challenges placed before her."

Personally, I think that the jury's still out on that. But then, that's one of the reasons that I'd relocated to a corporate city like Nevis Corners. The other reason stemmed from being closer to Nuclegene Corporation's cancer treatment center.

The center that had been destroyed just days ago.

"Are you ready, Logan?"

I looked up to see Maria holding a telltale syringe in one hand.

"Come on, let's hook you up to an IV drip," she said. "We'll set you up on the couch so you can watch TV. But if the company arrives before we're done, I'll move you into the bedroom."

"Thanks for doing this, Maria," I said.

Her worried expression spoke volumes to me.

"Sure. I just hope you know what you're doing."

"Hey, you're the PA here, not me," I quipped.

She rolled her eyes at me as she prepared the IV on my left arm.

"Right now, we're far outside of physician's assistant territory," she said.

It seemed as if I'd sat on her couch for a lifetime as the mysterious clear liquid slowly filtered into my body.

To pass the time, we chatted about Maria's twelve-year-old daughter, Lauren, and her eight-year-old son, Todd. She confided in me about how difficult it'd been to raise two children on her own in the two years since her divorce. Apparently, her ex, Mark, lived in nearby Des Moines and only visited the kids a few times per year.

In all the months I'd visited the treatment center, this

was the first time I truly felt like I was getting to know Maria as a person rather than the PA who administered my treatment.

It felt real and sincere; simply two people getting to know each other.

It felt good.

Maria recounted how she'd changed her original college major from chemical engineering to medicine about halfway through her degree program because she wanted to be more directly involved in caring for patients rather than being stuck in a laboratory.

Then the topic changed from the uncertainty of her career with Nuclegene to the friends and co-workers she'd lost in the explosion. I got the definite impression that recent revelations regarding the true nature of Nuclegene's cancer treatments had given her pause to doubt her employer.

The truth was, I had my doubts, too.

A couple of hours later, Maria removed the IV from my arm, marking it as what I intended to be my final treatment. Frankly, that prospect felt pretty good.

"Remember, as far as I'm concerned, this never happened," she insisted.

"Got it. How long do you think it'll take before we know something?" I asked, lightly massaging the small bandaged spot on my arm.

"Hard to say for certain. Perhaps a week," she said with a shrug. "In the meantime, call me if you have any complications or feel concerned about any side effects."

I nodded. "I'm already concerned about the side effects."

"Drink lots of fluids to build up your electrolytes," she suggested. "That's your body's key fuel for your abilities. And keep practicing your skills. I recall that one of the doctor's journal entries hypothesized that, just as with learning complex math or martial arts, concentration and repetition should strengthen the control and scope of your abilities."

"Thanks, I'll do that," I said as I turned to leave.

"And, Logan, please be careful," she warned. "There's

no way to determine how advanced your abilities may become, or how stable they'll be."

"Careful is my middle name," I assured her with a grin.

"Why am I having such a hard time believing that?" she asked.

I spied the mischievous look on her face and winked.

That evening, I fell asleep with no difficulty whatsoever. However, I woke up around four in the morning bathed in a cold sweat. My body felt achy and hot, almost feverish, so I took a shower.

For the first time, I compelled the soap to leap into my palm with little effort. I did the same with the bath towel hung over the shower door. Better, yet, I was able to fling the towel from my hand. It slapped against the mirror as if it had been thrown!

After nearly an hour of playing around with either retrieving or repelling various objects around the house, my body felt weak and my mind flustered. I wandered into the kitchen to pour a large glass of Gatorade.

Three glasses later, I felt somewhat refreshed and reenergized. Maria's hypothesis regarding replenishing electrolytes seemed to be correct.

I couldn't help feeling that things like this only happened in comic books; though I scarcely felt like superhero material.

* * *

On Tuesday and Wednesday evenings, and in the privacy of my home, I practiced moving objects both large and small. For the first time in recent memory, I was actually excited about something, and I practiced relentlessly. Maybe it had been the results of my additional treatment on Monday evening, but my progress was shocking.

By Wednesday night, I'd managed to push the dining room furniture across the room, resulting in a throbbing headache afterward. To my relief, I discovered that replenishing my body's electrolytes with sports drinks reduced my fatigue and lessened the severity of the headaches.

The probing of my limitations revealed a number of unexpected capabilities. While bouncing a small rubber ball against my living room wall one evening, I spontaneously generated an invisible "shield" that kept me from injuring an eye from a wayward bounce.

With practice, I gained a nuanced proficiency in shifting small objects or substances around. Granted, I was using hand gestures as the focal point for my actions like some stage magician, but I did manage to swirl a stack of magazines, newspapers, and a layer of furniture dust into midair, as well as relocate a cloud of steam across the bathroom that I had generated from my hot shower.

Hell, I was playing around just like a kid on summer vacation; but to be honest, it was the most fun that I'd had in a long time.

CHAPTER 5

By Thursday, I felt confident that I could push somebody over with my newly-refined skills. Still, nothing beat actual physical exercise; the feeling of endorphins surging through my body was invigorating.

Some people were runners, but I preferred jogging immediately following a workday, typically during early evenings. I'd given up that oh-dark-thirty morning workout crap when I left the army. Nowadays, I alternated days between jogging and weight lift training.

Whether jogging or lifting weights, both were great for working off the day's stress. I'd converted one of the spare bedrooms into a weight room, but I did my jogging in the elaborate park located in the heart of our model corporate city.

I had to admit, Nevis Corners was a nice city, despite having been co-sponsored by a consortium of some of the largest profit-hungry corporations. Frankly, a number of the nation's shrewdest corporations seemed to be at the center of all the major political and financial corruptions of the past few decades. Still, the politicians catered to them as if they were family.

Hell, I still remembered a few years back when one boastful ultra-conservative senator even tried to sell the idea that corporations were just like *people*.

What an asshole.

Half of the world's economy was in the shitter, and it seemed as if the only people hurting in our nation were the breathing kind. Meanwhile, the "corporation people" were wallowing in cash reserves and not creating much in the way of jobs for us "breathing people."

At least I had a steady job at the tag agency.

Count your blessings, they say.

During the second mile of my jog, my cell phone rang. I paused and looked down at the phone's screen.

Out of area.

"Hello?" I answered, catching my breath.

"Hello, Bringer," replied a gruff male voice.

"Who is this?"

"The time's come for you to start making choices," he said. "Preferably, smarter ones. The less that you discuss with the FBI, the better."

"And just why should I take advice from some asshole with no name?"

The guy chuckled in a way that oozed self-satisfaction, which annoyed me to no end.

"I think it's important to keep those close to you safe, don't you?"

My throat tightened.

"That so? Maybe you'd like to convey that in person?"

The only response was silence.

Jerking the phone from my ear, I quickly realized that the connection had ceased.

Given my sister's proximity, my first thought was of her. I immediately dialed her house, but got no answer. I glanced at my watch, realizing it was relatively close to dinnertime for them.

I tried both Lexi's and her husband's cell phone, but still got no answer. That worried me...a lot. I think that I broke an Olympic record running the distance back to my Dodge Avenger.

The tires squealed as I jammed the gearshift into drive and floored the accelerator. I weaved in and out of traffic like a madman, all the while trying to get hold of my sister's home or cell.

I tried Kevin's cell again, to no avail.

As I cut around a slower vehicle and sped through a series of stoplights, I resolved that my typical fifteen-minute drive was going to end ten minutes earlier. Five minutes later, I heard the sounds of sirens somewhere nearby, and a sense of dread set in.

Conjuring years of self-discipline, I focused on the task before me. All I knew was I had to get to my sister's house.

After what felt like forever, I rounded a corner and careened into my sister's addition. It was then that I saw the black smoke billowing ahead into the early evening sky.

God, please.

That surprised me. I hadn't pleaded to Him for anything in a long time.

By the time I made it to my sister's street, a sick feeling had already formed in the pit of my stomach. I could see reddish-yellow flames and black smoke pouring out of the roof of Lexi's two-story house.

A small group of people were gathered in the front yard. It looked like my brother-in-law and my little nephew, Jake, were among them. Both were on their hands and knees coughing. Neighbors appeared to be tending to them the best that they could.

I ran my car up into their neighbor's empty front yard, and catapulted out of the driver's seat to rush over to Kevin.

"Kevin! Where are Lexi and Kristie?"

Kevin hacked like some chain smoker at the end of his rope and shook his head.

"Still inside," he gasped. "Going for them next..."

The sounds of sirens permeated the air, though it was of little solace. I had no intentions of waiting on them.

"Stay here," I ordered.

I flew onto the porch at a dead run, impacting a wall of

angry black smoke as I entered the front door. My mind reeled as I tried to figure out where they might be.

"Lexi! Kristie!" I yelled.

I coughed and immediately realized that I didn't have much time. The roar of flames and a wall of heat loomed toward the kitchen to my left. I tried to visualize the layout of the house as I reasoned where they might be.

Then something strange and alien triggered in my mind, though it felt like nothing more than an insistent notion; an epiphany.

No, it felt like *certainty*.

Upstairs.

I concentrated on controlling my breathing and ducked low, focused on making it up the stairs. I felt raging heat at my back and realized that the living room had just been engulfed by flames.

As I hit the top of the stairs, I saw doorways lining both sides of the hallway.

Right side.

It was as if I could *feel* their minds nearby.

I crouched low to the floor but there wasn't much more air than at walking height. I refused to let a fresh spasm of coughing deter my efforts to spring forward into the first open room that I came to.

It was Kristie's bedroom, and both she and Lexi were lying on the floor coughing uncontrollably.

"Lexi! Kristie!" I yelled, slamming the bedroom door shut behind me.

Lexi seemed only half-conscious, but she appeared to recognize me.

"Logan," she gasped.

I heard a muffled roar and looked back toward the bedroom door, seeing the paint bubbling across its surface.

I quickly considered the bedroom window, which was shut tight. A growing sense of doom welled in me as I realized we were all going to die unless we managed to get the hell out of the house.

No time for doubts. Playtime was over.

Recalling my recent game of bouncing a ball against the wall, I tried to imagine a small wrecking ball as I jammed the flat of my hand toward the window. I felt a rush of adrenaline through my body and my head felt like it was going to split in half.

To my amazement, the entire window exploded outward in a shower of glass and metal framing. Saving my awe for later, I dragged Lexi and Kristie over to the opening in the wall that was formerly the window. I hoisted Kristie's petite body up and passed her out onto the shingled roof.

As I gasped for breath and reached down for Lexi, a fireman seemed to materialize from nowhere just outside the window.

He hoisted Kristie onto his right shoulder and yelled, "Hey, they're up here!"

A roar sounded behind me, and I felt flames nearly upon my back as I struggled to half-shove, half-throw my sister through the window. Fortunately, another fireman was already waiting there to take her from me.

My mind clouded and I dropped to the floor in a fit of coughing. I felt so drained and lifeless at that moment, as if all of the energy in my body had been sapped.

At least I'd helped save Lexi and Kristie.

That's when I felt my body being lifted from the floor.

"C'mon, mister!" a man's muffled voice challenged. "We ain't losing anybody today!"

With his help, I struggled to make it out onto the roof. The fireman only barely managed to make it out himself before the flames shot out through the shattered window.

My lucky day, I guessed.

The next thing I knew, I was on the grass of the front yard with an oxygen mask pressed to my face. A host of curious neighbors, firemen, police, and even a few television reporters milled around the area. I stared up at the house and could tell that the structure was destined to be a complete loss.

Well, not a complete loss. I still have my family.

Then the mysterious caller from the park came to the forefront of my mind, and anger swelled within me.

I didn't know who was out to harm my family, but I vowed that somebody's days were definitely numbered. Nobody threatened my family like that and got away with it.

By the time the oxygen did its work on me, Lexi and the kids were being transported to the local hospital. Kevin rode with them, so I was left alone to stare at the still-smoldering remains of their home.

My head ached terribly and I still felt weak, as if I'd just completed a marathon.

A police officer walked over to take my statement on the incident, and I wrestled with whether or not to tell them about my mysterious phone call.

My thoughts were interrupted by the arrival of Agent Megan Sanders in a black Toyota Camry, sans her partner. She strode purposefully over to me and took a moment to survey the scene before her.

"And what brought you so quickly over to your sister's house?" asked the officer as he cast a quick glance over his shoulder to where deep ruts lead to my hastily abandoned vehicle. Somebody had been kind enough to turn off the ignition, I noticed.

I stood to look directly into Agent Sanders' eyes instead of the officer's. "I got a strange phone call."

Sanders' eyes widened slightly, and she quickly turned her attention to the officer.

"Officer, this is an FBI matter. I'll finish taking Mr. Bringer's statement."

He appeared surprised but then he shrugged.

"Okay with me," he said before turning to walk over to where a fellow officer was addressing a growing crowd of onlookers.

"So, where's your other half?" I quipped.

She glanced at her watch. "Probably home with his family by now."

"So, you're the workaholic of the pair then?" I asked, rubbing at my eyes with my fingertips. My head was pounding.

"Something like that," she replied, quirking her lips. "Mr. Bringer, shouldn't you have gone to the hospital?"

"I'm fine, thanks. I've got a wicked headache, that's all."

"Let's talk about your phone call at our office downtown," she suggested.

"I'd love to," I said. "But first, you're going to have to let me grab a change of clothes from my house."

"Fine," she agreed. "But I think I'll drive," she added, noticing my car's chaotically parked condition.

Sanders called her partner, Agent Burroughs, on the way to my place, and he agreed to meet us there for some strange reason.

"Why, Agent Sanders, I might think that you don't entirely trust me," I said.

She appeared amused. "Just standard procedure, Mr. Bringer."

I pointed to a convenience store ahead.

"Hey, can you pull in there? I really could use something to drink, and maybe come aspirin."

"Um, sure," she said, a peculiar expression adorning her face.

She accompanied me into the store, and the cashier observed us with a strange look on his face. I was sure that it wasn't every day that he saw a soot-covered man in jogging attire being accompanied by a lady in a business suit.

Before we even made it back to her car, I had downed over half the container of Gatorade and popped two aspirins.

Within minutes, the pounding in my head abated considerably, and I felt renewed energy course through my body. Maria Edwards had been right on the money concerning my body's need for electrolytes. The brief use of my abilities at my sister's house had taken quite a toll on me.

Ten minutes later, we arrived at my house across town. For the most part, my body already felt surprisingly rejuvenated.

A plain-looking, black four-door sedan was already parked in my driveway, which must've been Agent Burroughs'. However, there remained enough ambient light to discern from the street that my front door appeared to be ajar.

"My front door is open," I said to Agent Sanders as we exited her car. "I know that I locked it before I left to go jogging earlier this evening."

Sanders reached to her right hip to place a hand on her automatic pistol. "Stay here," she ordered as she drew her weapon.

She peered around the corner of my house to the front porch and quickly made her way to my front door.

"FBI. Agent Burroughs, are you in there?" she demanded authoritatively.

As I peered around the brick facade to the front porch, I heard a slight moaning sound.

"Burroughs!" Sanders shouted.

She crouched down next to the prone form of her partner, who was lying on his back in my living room not far from the door. I started in that direction, but spied somebody to the left via my peripheral vision.

I turned to my left just in time to see a tall man with closely-cropped red hair and wearing a black London Fog coat peer from around the far side of my house. His hands flew upward, and I saw a pistol with silencer being aimed directly at me.

"This is Agent Sanders with the FBI. We have an agent down with multiple gunshot wounds at…" Sanders rattled off on her cell phone, oblivious to what was transpiring.

I felt my heart stop as I instinctively raised my right palm up to shield me, for all the good it would do. It sounded like a miniature air gun belched, and my mind felt like it had been struck by two heavy hammers.

As the stranger disappeared around the corner of my house, I focused upon two small copper objects that were suspended in mid-air just beyond my palm.

Bullets!

My eyes widened and the two small objects fell harmlessly to the concrete sidewalk amidst subdued clinking noises.

Agent Sanders launched out onto the front porch with her weapon drawn, staring at me in disbelief. She pivoted in the direction of where my assailant had been standing, and rapidly closed the distance to the corner of the house.

Despite the throbbing pain in my forehead, I rushed forward to follow her.

Sanders had already made her way down the length of the side of my house and was leaping over the top of the low vinyl fence surrounding my back yard by the time that I rounded the corner.

I continued after her at a dead run. Sanders stopped in the middle of my yard, scanning the darkness of the tree line at the back of my property as a multitude of sirens wailed in the distance.

My mind *sensed* someone among the trees to the right, and I scarcely managed to focus upon a lone dark-clad figure standing there.

"To your right!" I shouted, as two muffled belches erupted in the silence.

My right palm was extended before I knew it; reflexes left over from combat experiences earned in the battlefield. Sanders' body tensed as I felt two more heavy thuds in my head, only this time they were followed by sharp, stabbing pains.

My vision blurred slightly, but I managed to focus on Sanders, who quickly scanned to her right. She gasped with shock and stared at two coppery objects suspended before her forehead.

She gasped as the small projectiles dropped harmlessly to the ground before her.

The moment seemed frozen in time, save for a breeze rustling the trees before us and the louder wail of approaching sirens. Despite the throbbing in my head, I no longer *sensed* the presence of anyone else immediately around us.

After scanning the area with her pistol held before her, Sanders turned to face me with an astonished expression.

"Are you—? Did you—?"

I rubbed at my throbbing temples, relieved that she hadn't been injured. The fact that I'd been able to stop those bullets from hitting her meant more to me than I'd expected. A wave of confusion coursed through me, battling for supremacy with the effects of exhaustion and an adrenaline rush.

"It's complicated," I said.

I felt something trickling from my nose and brushed my fingers across the spot. My nose was bleeding.

She lowered her weapon and rushed past me toward the front of my house.

"Burroughs," she muttered.

Three police officers had their guns drawn on us as soon as we rounded the corner. Fortunately, Agent Sanders already had her badge out.

"FBI, Agent Sanders," she announced authoritatively. "There's a gunman in the area; tall and wearing a dark fog coat. He fled south through the trees at the back of the house."

Two officers immediately headed in that direction while the other scanned the immediate area. Fire department paramedics were already tending to Agent Burroughs as an ambulance pulled up to the curb before my house.

I felt dizzy and squatted on the ground to dab at my bleeding nose as Sanders watched over the ministrations to her partner.

It'd turned into one hell of a day.

* * *

Two hours later, I marveled at the control that a single

FBI agent seemed to have over the crime scene. Agent Sanders had somehow managed to remove an entire set of my clothes from my home, claiming it was for "evidence", which I genuinely appreciated.

Despite her obvious concern for her partner, who'd been transported to the same local hospital where my sister and her family had been taken, Sanders appeared remarkably calm and composed as she drove us downtown to the high-rise building housing the local FBI office.

Their office area was surprisingly modern-looking, and I was only too pleased to be offered the use of a walk-in shower in an oversized private lavatory. I appreciated the hot shower, which granted me the first opportunity that evening to reflect on all that had happened.

I was having difficulty putting the self-evident puzzle pieces together, struggling to determine who might be at the center of events that had transpired.

Granted, divining mysteries such as that wasn't something I was used to doing, but there was more to it than that.

Maybe it was the continued pounding in my head, or the aching in my body, or even the lingering adrenaline coursing through my system that kept me from thinking entirely clearly. Either way, I quickly realized that I was severely lacking enough information to make even a wild-ass guess.

After cleaning up and changing into fresh clothes, I returned to the main office area. The place was buzzing with the activities of half a dozen agents.

I spotted Agent Sanders and made my way to her. She looked up at me with a penetrating expression and gestured to a spare chair before her desk. To my surprise, there was already a cold container of a sports drink waiting for me.

Apparently, she remembered my drink of choice.

"Feel better?" she asked. "Your nose stopped bleeding, I see."

"Yeah, thanks," I replied. Then I reconsidered her question. "Actually, that's not entirely true. To feel 'better' would require that I wasn't pissed off that someone tried to kill me and members of my family."

She nodded but stared at me warily.

"Who are you exactly, Logan Bringer?" she asked. "I've never seen anything like what I saw happen this evening."

I drew in a deep breath and slowly exhaled, wishing that I had proper answers for her, and for myself.

"Yeah, I'm still coming to grips with that myself," I replied. "Two weeks ago, I'd have said that I was just some lucky schmuck who managed to live through brain cancer. But today…hell if I know."

She'd asked a fair question, really.

Who am I? What am I?

An uncomfortable silence grew between us, and no less than two agents slowed as they passed Sanders' desk, each openly staring at me with mixed degrees of curiosity.

"Thank you," Sanders offered in a quiet voice.

I looked into her hazel eyes with surprise, and then realized what she'd meant.

The bullets.

I felt really good about what I'd managed to do, and I couldn't keep from breaking into a wan smile.

"You're welcome."

She was the first to break eye contact, instead glancing down to some printouts before her. She had beautiful eyes.

I opened the sports drink and started chugging. Unfortunately, the sweetness of the liquid was mixed with the lingering taste of ash and smoke. That aside, I quickly appreciated the subsiding pain and aching in my head within a matter of minutes.

Electrolytes; my newest little friends.

"What happens next?" I asked.

"Procedures dictate—" she started to say but stopped midsentence.

She sighed. "Actually, Mr. Bringer, I'm afraid that we're way outside standard operating procedures right now."

Something in the back of my mind sensed she was

distracted, almost as if torn between decisions at that moment. Frankly, I found her indecision mildly comforting; I wasn't the only person who felt completely out of their element.

Difficult circumstances were more bearable when shared.

"How's Agent Burroughs?" I asked.

Her expression darkened.

"He's in surgery right now."

I nodded. "Listen, Agent Sanders, both of us have people we care about at the hospital right now. Maybe we'd be best served there."

I thought I caught a brief flash of relief cross her face before she composed herself again, back to the ever-clinical looking FBI agent.

"Okay, we can talk about that phone call you received earlier this evening on the way there," she conceded.

"Sure," I said.

"Then maybe you'll tell me a little bit more about how you came to stop bullets in mid-air," she added in a subdued tone.

"I'm afraid that's a bit more incredible," I said.

"Try me. I have a fluid imagination," she countered with an arched brow.

I was beginning to like Agent Sanders in ways that I hadn't expected.

CHAPTER 6

By the time we reached the hospital, I'd described to Sanders some of the abilities I'd developed since my last treatment. To say that she'd appeared surprised bordering on disbelief was an understatement. Somehow, I got the impression that if she hadn't seen the bullets suspended in midair before her, she'd have immediately delivered me to the Guthrie County Psychiatric Hospital.

I finished describing the mysterious phone call that I'd received at the park as we pulled into the hospital parking lot. Sanders remained silent, appearing contemplative, as we strode through the emergency entrance.

I followed her to one of the hospital's surgical waiting areas, which frankly reminded me of an oversized doctor's office waiting room. Though a number of people were present, a worried-looking woman who appeared to be in her thirties immediately caught my attention. Beside her were two young girls who were almost spitting images of her, each with a head of blonde hair.

Sanders strode immediately to the woman, who rose to embrace her.

"Sally, I'm so sorry," she said. "How're you and the kids holding up? Has anyone met with you yet?"

Sally appeared to struggle to hold back a wave of tears.

"We're doing the best we can," she replied in a near whisper.

Sanders took a moment to simultaneously hug the girls, one under each arm. It was apparent that she cared a great deal not only her partner but for his family.

I sighed. Waiting rooms always brimmed with an aura of helplessness, anticipation, and sometimes dread.

My mind quickly gravitated to my own family, who were located somewhere else in the hospital. I turned to address Sanders, but she was already glancing at me with a somber expression.

"Go. I'll come find you later," she said.

I nodded and made my way to the nearest information desk.

* * *

Two hours passed before I finished my visit with Lexi, Kevin, and the kids. I was so relieved that they hadn't been seriously harmed. Lexi and Kristie had suffered minor smoke inhalation, but were expected to be released by morning.

Unfortunately, I learned very little about the fire. As far as they knew, it seemed to erupt spontaneously somewhere near the kitchen or utility room.

"I guess I'd better call Mom and Dad," I ventured.

"Too late. I already called them," Lexi said with a smirk.

I couldn't help but chuckle at my sister's innate sense of efficiency despite her distress. With a final hug, I insisted I had to meet with the authorities further. Lexi knew that I'd already been interviewed by the police and FBI following the explosion at the Wallace Building.

"Wait, Logan," Lexi insisted. "Does somebody think that our fire was somehow related to your case?"

I did the only thing that seemed sensible at that moment. I lied.

"Nah, I think they just want to go over some additional details, that's all," I reassured her.

There didn't seem to be any point in worrying them when I didn't have all the facts myself. What was I supposed to tell them, anyway? *Sure, Lexi, mysterious people from God-knows-where are out to get my family and me, but there's nothing to worry about.*

Lexi frowned at my response but let it drop. I signaled to Kevin to follow me into the hallway as I made my way out. As soon as we closed the door to Lexi's room, I turned to him.

"Listen, I don't have all the details just yet, but maybe this is a good time for you to take Lexi and the kids to my Mom and Dad's for a visit."

Besides being a hell of a talented architect, Kevin was a good man and a great father and husband. He looked me in the eye as if patiently assessing me and nodded.

"You think this is related, don't you?" he asked.

"Honestly, Kev, there's a crap-load of stuff that I don't know yet," I replied. "But you can damn well bet I'm getting to the bottom of things *real soon*. Right now, my highest priority is to make sure that you, Lexi, and the kids are safe. And right now, your safest place may not be in Nevis Corners."

I could almost see the wheels turning in his brain as he pursed his lips. Then he nodded.

"The kids could stand to miss a few days of school anyway, given what just happened," he temporized. "And Lexi needs a few days to rest, according to the doctor. But if I know her, she'd just run herself ragged trying to sort through the mess at the house. For that alone, being out of town is definitely a good idea."

"Don't worry. I've got some good friends who can go over to help out with the house," I said.

My friend Travis could see to that. The guy was like a walking Swiss Army knife; he had a solution for every situation.

"Yeah, I've already received a call back from my brother and sister-in-law who pretty much said the same thing," he agreed.

We shook hands like two men who had just agreed on a business deal or something.

"Logan, be careful, and let us know as soon as you learn anything," Kevin insisted.

I nodded and headed down the hallway to the elevators. In the midst of the chaos, it felt good to experience a momentary glimmer of encouragement. For some reason, just like back in Afghanistan a few years ago, I felt like I was conducting damage control in a war zone.

By the time that I made my way back to the waiting room where I'd left Agent Sanders, both she and the other family members were gone. A quick consultation at the information desk confirmed that Burroughs had already been moved to a room upstairs. At least that meant he'd survived his surgery.

"Logan!"

I turned to see Maria Edwards briskly walking down the hallway toward me.

"Maria? What are you doing here?"

"I saw the news report on TV about the fire at your sister's house," she explained. "They reported that some people had been transported to the hospital. There's also a story about a shooting in your neighborhood."

"The press must be having a field day. Nevis Corners has practically turned into an action film," I murmured.

"Yeah, well, it probably won't take long for the press to correlate the two events as being related to you and your family. Then they'll tie your affiliation to the Nuclegene bombing."

Good point.

"Yeah, great," I said. "But why are you here?"

She paused and pulled me into a nearby unoccupied family conference room and closed the door behind us.

"I'd hoped that I'd find you here," she said. "Logan, I've been reading through more of the information that I downloaded from Nuclegene's systems regarding your treatments. One of the researchers hypothesized that there might be a way to refine your abilities."

"And you couldn't wait to tell me *because*?" I asked.

"As soon as I saw the news footage showing the ragged opening around your sister's upstairs window, I suspected that you'd harnessed your abilities further. Nobody kicks part of a wall and brick facade out, no matter how much adrenaline is flowing in their system. Then, when I heard about a shooting at your home, I thought that somebody must be after you. Logan, I felt that I had to try and help you somehow."

I appreciated that she cared enough to try and help me so much.

"Tell me what you discovered."

She extracted a small syringe of clear fluid from her purse and held it up.

"I acquired the base elements from a nutrition center in town and then combined them into a liquid form. There's a combination of extracts, including Taurine, L-Carnitine, Ginseng, L-theanine, and Inositol. Together, they're supposed to enhance vital chemical processes in your brain that strengthen and refine your abilities. Oh, and there's a spectrum of B vitamins to boost your body's energy levels, as well."

I stared at her as if she were a mad scientist.

"I was a chemistry major, remember? Look, I went to a lot of trouble here," she said with a stony expression. "Do you want my help or not?"

One thing was certain; I needed my abilities to be as sharp and strong as possible for what may lie ahead. I pulled my shirtsleeve up over my shoulder and she rubbed an alcohol wipe across my skin. Then she injected the entire contents of the syringe into my arm.

"There. If this works, you should begin to feel the effects within the next few hours," she advised.

I nodded and then adopted a mischievous expression.

"Speaking of abilities, you wanna' hear something

interesting?" I baited.

After I'd described what had transpired at my home with the bullets, she plopped down into one of the nearest cushioned chairs with a shocked expression.

"My God, Logan," she finally said. "I've never heard of anything like that before. Of course, there's certainly nothing in the medical records about any previous patients doing anything like that."

"Thankfully everything worked; although I experienced a brief nose bleed after I stopped the second set of bullets," I added.

She considered my statement with a grim expression.

"There's some kind of force-feedback taking place," she estimated. "Logan, there's no telling what kind of damage that might cause to your brain."

"Do you think that the nosebleeds might stop if my abilities continue to strengthen?" I pressed.

She appeared deep in thought at length before finally shaking her head.

"Honestly, I have no idea," she admitted. "These are all cutting-edge experiences now. You're likely the first person who's advanced this far into their abilities before, though I'd have to search Nuclegene's entire database to know for certain."

I nodded. Then I looked down at her with appreciation.

"I can't thank you enough for helping me, Maria," I offered.

Her resulting smile was a movie-star-worthy level of spectacular. Her eyes darted to her watch and she quickly rose from the chair.

"I have to return home. My neighbor, Claire, was kind enough to watch the kids for me, but I really need to get back to them now," she explained. "I'll start making more of the liquefied supplement for you as soon as possible."

I bent over and gently pressed a quick kiss to her cheek.

"Thank you for everything," I offered. "I'll keep you posted."

She nodded and then we both went our separate ways.

I continued to the fifth floor and located Burroughs' room by the sight of his daughters sitting nearby in an oversized family waiting area that served as a central lobby for the patient's rooms in that wing of the building. I looked at the nurse's station to see both Sally Burroughs and Agent Sanders meeting with a doctor.

"Are you here to help Aunt Meg find the person who shot my daddy?" asked one of the girls.

Aunt Meg?

Then I remembered Agent Sanders' business card.

Megan Sanders.

I stared at the innocent face of one of the blonde-haired, blue-eyed girls who couldn't have been more than five or six years old. Burroughs might be an asshole, but his daughters seemed like little angels.

I squatted down to see her eye-to-eye and adopted a reassuring expression.

"I'm certainly going to try," I said with as much resoluteness as I could muster.

An unusual bond had been formed by circumstance; Burroughs and his family, and me and my family.

A nurse peeked out from Burroughs' room. "Is there a Logan Bringer out here?"

"I'm Logan Bringer," I said.

"Mr. Burroughs is asking for you," she said. "But he's very weak following his surgery, so I'd appreciate if you'd keep your visit brief."

"Is that you, Bringer? I heard your voice," Burroughs' strained weak, but still gruff, voice demanded. "Get in here."

Both the girls crowded in around me to stare into their father's room.

"Daddy's going to have a chat with the nice man and then you can both come give me a big hug," Burroughs whispered in an unusually friendly-sounding tone.

The girls both replied in unison, "Okay, Daddy."

Well, I'll be damned; the jerk actually had a heart.

Okay, maybe I was being the asshole just then.

I closed the door and looked at the formerly robust FBI agent, who now looked more like someone who'd only narrowly cheated death. I'd seen that look before on the battlefield more times than I could count. Frankly, I was impressed that the guy was even conscious after all that he'd just been through.

"Sit your ass down, Bringer," he demanded in a weak, groggy voice. He paused to take in a few breaths before adding, "Tell me what the hell...is going on."

It sounded like he was maintaining consciousness by sheer willpower alone.

I recounted what I'd told his partner earlier and briefly described what had taken place at my house, including our little "bullet experience."

Believe it or not, the guy actually seemed to be listening for a change. Or maybe he was just fighting unconsciousness.

He moved his head back into his pillow and stared at the ceiling for what seemed like an eternity.

"Damn. I've never even heard of anything like that," he half-whispered. "Whatever this is, you're in deep, Bringer. And this better mean that you're planning to cooperate fully with us now."

"Just so long as I'm able to get to the bottom of who set fire to my sister's house and nearly killed my family."

Burroughs remained silent for a time.

"Fine. You can start by telling me why some heavy was ransacking your house when I arrived there."

"*Ransacking?*" I asked.

Burroughs took a series of shallow breaths before speaking again.

"Yeah, I heard him rifling through things. I think I surprised him, but he was a much quicker draw than me."

Burroughs closed his eyes for a few moments, and I almost got up to leave before he finally added, "My pistol barely cleared leather before I had two rounds in my chest."

I mulled that over for a moment. I wondered if the

stranger fired two rounds as a matter of habit.

Something about the technique triggered in my mind.

"This guy sounds like a pro. Maybe ex-special forces or sniper," I ventured aloud.

That realization should've made me cringe, but instead all that I felt was steely resolve.

"The man's formidable," Burroughs conceded.

"Doesn't matter," I added. "Soon, he'll be the one who needs to start looking over his shoulder."

Burroughs grunted.

"Well-well, I'd say that soldier boy finally woke up again," he whispered.

There were a few moments of shallow breaths before he spoke again.

"Honestly, when I first saw you, I thought you were just another washed-up, former army loser. What do you think about that, ground-pounder?"

I frowned.

"I think I'll let my future actions do the talking," I replied.

He squeezed his eyes shut and then opened them to stare at the ceiling above.

"Good enough for me, Army. Just don't get Sanders killed in the process, or so help me, I'll hunt you down if it's the last thing I do."

The guy was barely conscious and had numerous tubes stuck in his arms, yet he sounded like he meant every word.

"I stopped two bullets for her earlier tonight," I said. "What makes you think I won't stop more for her, if needed?"

The resulting surprised expression on his face was truly priceless.

A knock sounded behind me and the door opened to reveal both Agent Sanders and Burroughs' wife.

"Are we interrupting anything important?" Sanders asked with a suspicious expression.

"Nah," Burroughs insisted in a voice that sounded a little

weaker than a few minutes ago. "Just asking Bringer some questions."

"My God, Ted, you just got out of a critical surgery. I think you need to concentrate on healing for the time being," Sally Burroughs chastised. "However, you have two daughters who'd like to visit their father before you get some sleep."

Burroughs grunted.

I rubbed at my mouth with one hand to hide my look of amusement. It appeared that Agent Burroughs wasn't the only assertive person in their household.

"All right, honey," Burroughs muttered. "Come on in, girls."

His two daughters carefully squeezed past me and slowly approached their father's bedside. Agent Sanders gently led me from the room and toward the nearest elevators.

"Why in God's name were you pestering Agent Burroughs?" she asked in an accusatory tone.

"I couldn't resist the temptation," I replied dryly.

She shook her head but didn't press the subject.

"How's your family?" she asked as we entered the empty elevator car together.

"They're okay, thanks for asking. I suggested they should visit my parents out of town for a few days," I replied.

"Not a bad idea, but the police will want to visit with them first, myself included," she said.

I nodded.

"Where to now?" I asked.

Sanders pressed the button for the bottom floor.

"Back to our offices," she said. "We need to go over some more details and try to put together as many of the pieces to this puzzle as possible."

"We?"

She tentatively looked over at me.

"Mr. Bringer, it seems that you're at the center of everything on this case. Who better than you to help me work through things?"

"Fair enough, but there's something else that you need to do for me first," I stipulated.

She appeared surprised and her eyes narrowed. "And what exactly is that?"

I grinned despite myself.

"I'd consider it a courtesy if you'd start calling me Logan."

"I'll consider it, Mr. Bringer," she replied as we exited the elevator.

CHAPTER 7

Events had transpired so quickly and chaotically that I'd barely glanced at my watch since jogging earlier that evening. By the time I finally slouched into a cheap cushioned chair before Agent Sanders' desk at the FBI offices, it was nearly midnight. Remarkably, aside from being a little hungry, I felt surprisingly awake and alert.

The office still buzzed with four other agents who were busy either talking on the phone or working at computer terminals.

A female agent with long blonde hair suspiciously peered at me while she was on the phone. I politely looked away, and noticed Sanders staring at me, as well.

"Hungry?" she asked.

"Well, now that you mention it, yeah," I replied.

A few minutes later, a fellow wearing dark slacks and a blazer walked by and slipped two wrapped deli sandwiches and cans of Coca-Cola onto Sanders' desk.

"Thank you, sir," she said while smiling back at me.

"You earned it tonight," he replied as he strode across the room and into a small office.

I shook my head. "Now you're a mind reader?"

"Logical deduction," she replied.

"Your boss?" I asked, reaching for one of the

sandwiches.

"Chuck Denton. He's our field office supervisor," she replied as she popped the tab on her soda can.

For more than an hour, we went back over everything that I could recall, beginning with my jogging and leading through the fire at my sister's, and then of course, the shooting at my house.

As Sanders left her desk to visit with her boss, I yawned and was thinking that I needed my abilities to get a hell of a lot stronger if I was going to be of any use in defending my family.

Following that, I must've dozed off.

I thought that I was dreaming, but then, everything seemed so real and vivid. I sat in a crowded bus terminal, but it seemed too quiet given all of the people milling around me. When I scanned people's faces, they all silently stared back at me, and I recognized each of them. They were people who I'd seen that evening: firemen, police, hospital workers, and the agents in the field office, including Sanders.

Gradually, I heard some people talking in hushed tones. I looked around but only saw lips moving for the people representing the agents who were in the field office.

"Kind of a cute guy in the chair over there," the blonde-haired agent muttered.

"…help but wonder what his story is," another agent muttered.

"Do I dare tell Chuck about the bullets floating in midair?" Agent Sanders asked.

"Mayhem means nothing but endless overtime," another agent muttered sitting close by.

"I'll probably have to call in for additional agents on this case," Chuck Denton noted with aggravation from a bench seat across from me.

I woke up with a start and nearly fell out of my chair. Three agents arrayed around the room stared at me with a look of surprise.

I rubbed at my forehead and felt cool sweat on my palm.

"What the—?"

What's his problem?

...kind of an odd situation. I wonder what his story is.

There were voices in my head!

I looked over at the blonde-haired agent a few feet away and she stared back at me suspiciously.

I wonder if he's single?

"What?" I asked her.

She frowned. "I didn't say anything."

What's happening out there, said Sanders' voice in my head.

"What's wrong?" Sanders asked as she strode over to me.

"Whaddya' mean?" I asked, completely focused on her face.

What just happened, I could hear Sanders ask, except that her lips never moved!

"Everything's just fine," I insisted. "Just a weird dream. Must've nodded off."

She regarded me dubiously. Suddenly, I couldn't hear her thoughts anymore.

"Listen, it's been a long day for all of us. Let's call it a night and we'll pick up first thing in the morning," she suggested.

I nodded. "Sounds fine to me."

Sanders was kind enough to drop me back by my sister's home to retrieve my car. I noticed that there was a police car parked in the street, as well as someone from the fire department poking around with a flashlight. Crime tape was strewn about like a spider's web.

"I wouldn't try going to your home tonight," Sanders recommended. "It's going to be an active crime scene overnight. And I'll want some time to look over your place, as well. Get a hotel room."

I watched her drive away before noticing that my Dodge Avenger had been moved and was parked in the street in front of a neighbor's house. I read the note that had been tucked under the windshield wiper blade.

Mr. Bringer,

Your car is parked in front of our home and we're happy to give your keys to you when you're ready for them. Don't worry about how late it is when you come by.

Regards,
Beth and Joe Torrence

Lexi had friendly neighbors, and she'd always spoken highly of the Torrences. Despite what their note stated, I apologized to them for the late hour and promised to give their best wishes to my family.

I called Kevin and he told me that he, Lexi, and the kids were staying in a local hotel. With few other options myself, I stopped by a Walmart to purchase a fresh set of clothes and some personal items, and then stayed at the same hotel. It was somehow reassuring that I would be closer to my family in case they needed me.

Regardless of the late hour, my mother had left a couple of voicemails insisting that I call her immediately once I received her messages. To my surprise, she sounded wide awake when I called. I tried to reassure her that I was fine, and that most of all, Lexi, Kevin, and the kids were unharmed. Honestly, I've never worried as much about myself as others have. And, quite frankly, there's nothing like trying to convince your Mom at 2 a.m. that being involved in a house fire and a shooting in the same night was "nothing for her to worry about."

In fact, I had a hard time believing it myself.

* * *

The next morning, I called my boss, Larry Anderson, and briefly explained what had happened the previous evening. He'd seen the news and was more than willing to excuse me from work for a few days. Larry was someone you'd call "good people."

I'd barely been off the phone for two minutes before I received a call from my best friend, Travis, who'd also seen the stories on the local news and wanted far more details than I felt comfortable revealing. Given the violent nature of the mysterious assailants in my life, I somehow felt that it was probably safer for him if he knew less versus more.

I stopped by my sister's room to check on her and the kids. They planned to stop by their home in the morning just long enough to pick through some personal belongings and then travel to Mom and Dad's house. Somehow, Kevin had managed to sell Lexi on the plan, but I could tell that she was wrestling with herself over leaving with so many things left unattended. A part of me didn't want to see them go, either, but I couldn't watch over them while also delving further into whatever was going on.

A part of me wondered if my family would be safe merely leaving town, but there was little else that I could do, until either the authorities uncovered further evidence or I somehow single-handedly managed to bring additional evidence to light. That realization seemed insurmountable in my mind, but I forced such thoughts aside. It was precisely what my elusive "enemies" would want.

"I've got to at least be able to put a tangible *name* to these damned people," I muttered.

I'd just reached into my pocket for the keys and remote to my Dodge Avenger to head to a local cafe for some breakfast when Agent Sanders pulled up behind my vehicle and rolled down her window.

"Well, you're up early," she said. "How do you feel about a working breakfast?"

"Working? I'll have you know I've got the day off," I said.

"Correction, you *had* the day off," she said with wry expression.

The gleam in her hazel eyes appeared almost playful, and

I couldn't help but grin. Besides, who could resist an offer from a face like hers?

Not me.

"Working breakfast, eh? That's the best offer I've had all morning," I said and walked around to the passenger side of her car.

Within the hour, we sat at Sanders' desk eating breakfast. I eyed her all-organic bagel and yogurt as I spooned away at my Styrofoam container of hot oatmeal.

"Health food advocate?" I asked.

"Healthy body, healthy mind," she chirped, staring at the large bottle of sports drink before me. "Though oatmeal and Gatorade seems like an odd combination."

I had to admit that my new liquid dietary supplement was peculiar.

"Believe it or not, it's sort of the same for me," I hedged. "One for body, one for brain."

She frowned but didn't inquire further. For the time being, it was my own little inside joke.

"How's Agent Burroughs?" I asked.

"He's stable and resting comfortably," she replied simply. "His prognosis is good."

I nodded. "That's good news."

"We should probably go over events from yesterday one more time before we take a look around your house. The police said the interior had been rifled through," Sanders said in a voice that sounded once more like a practiced FBI agent; all business.

I must've been foggy-headed last night, because suddenly questions were clearly forming in my mind based upon what Sanders had just said.

"What was he looking for?" I asked.

"An excellent question," she said, spooning up the remainder of her yogurt. "However, the fact that your assailant tried to kill you suggests that maybe he'd found what he was looking for."

"Hm," I mumbled as I finished my oatmeal.

Then out of nowhere, it hit me what the visitor may have been seeking.

"We need to go to my house," I said.

"That's our next stop, in fact," she said.

Twenty minutes later, we pulled into my driveway. As with my sister's place, crime scene tape seemed chaotically strewn around and across the property. And I noticed that the deadbolt on my front door had been replaced with a new one. Fortunately, Sanders produced a shiny new key that opened it.

"Someone needs to give one of those to me," I said.

"Technically, it's still a crime scene, so you're not supposed to be coming and going," she stipulated. "In fact, don't take anything without asking me, either."

I grumbled as I followed her into *my* home. It was then that I appreciated how thoroughly the "rifling" had been. Furniture had been upturned everywhere, and a litany of personal belongings were haphazardly strewn about. I also noticed a bloody area on my living room carpet where Agent Burroughs had fallen.

Sanders' attention likewise seemed momentarily fixed upon that spot, as well.

"Do you immediately notice anything missing?" she asked, pulling open the drapes to allow natural light in.

I heaved a sigh as I surveyed many broken personal effects lying about. I entered my spare bedroom that I had turned into my hobby room. As I had expected, most of my meticulously-built models had been broken as they were cast aside. During the painstaking months of illness and treatments, particularly once I'd become physically debilitated, I'd resorted to building models to pass the time. Each model had served as my own therapeutic form of Bonsai tree, in fact.

Sanders appeared behind me in the doorway and reached down to pick up a model of NASA's Apollo 13 Lunar Lander.

"My brother, Tom, used to put models together," she

absently noted. "Like you, he was pretty good at it. Good representation of moon dirt marks on the pads."

I sifted through the near-debris that scattered the floor, and finally looked underneath a small shelf that had been tipped over against an open filing cabinet. I picked up the small wooden model of a 688 Attack Submarine and unscrewed the nosepiece. Inside was a handkerchief that had been rolled up around a USB memory drive.

Well, I'll be damned. The guy might just have left empty-handed, after all.

Sanders noticed the device in my hand. "A memory stick? Something important?" she asked.

For a moment, I half-considered lying, and telling her that it was just backups of my financial data or family photos. But somehow, I felt that if anybody could help me get to the bottom of what had been going on, it was likely Sanders. And to do that, she needed to know as much as I did.

At least, for the most part.

For some reason, there was something about her that seemed...trustworthy.

I looked her squarely in the eyes and she must've gauged what I'd been thinking.

"You can trust me, Logan," she assured me in what sounded like a sincere tone of voice.

The point wasn't lost on me that she'd at least used my first name.

She was either very sincere or very accomplished at subterfuge.

"The question is, do you trust me?" I asked.

"You mustn't be too evil of a guy. After all, you did save my life last night," she said. "And if I hadn't mentioned it yet, I really appreciate that. So does my family."

I felt a smile touch my lips.

"I was given this by someone who wanted me to know about the true nature of my treatments at the Nuclegene Cancer Center," I explained. "It contains clinical files that might help explain why I had the ability to stop those bullets in midair."

Sanders' eyebrows arched with curiosity.

"I've been toying with the idea that Nuclegene had more to do with everything that's happened," she said.

"So, you don't think that I'm a terrorist, then?" I asked.

"Well, I never said that. However, if you are, you don't seem like such a bad terrorist so far," she said in a mock-conspiratorial tone.

I winked back at her.

Then something about the memory drive caused something even darker to occur to me, and I immediately reached for my cell phone.

"Dammit!"

"What's wrong?" she asked.

"Whoever shot at us was probably looking for something like this," I hastily explained. "And I think I know who might be next on his list."

I cursed myself for not having thought of it last night.

"Hello?" answered a man's worried voice.

"Hello? Can I speak to Maria? It's urgent," I insisted.

"Who is this? If you've got anything to do with her disappearance, so help me—" the man threatened.

The sinking feeling in my stomach seemed bottomless. Someone had already gotten to her.

"Listen, my name is Logan Bringer and I'm a friend of Maria's. I'm here with the FBI. We're on our way over," I insisted.

Sanders' expression turned icy as I hung up the phone.

"Who was that, and what in the *hell* are you talking about?" she demanded.

"I'll explain everything, but you've got to trust me when I say that someone very innocent needs our help right now. I think that she may have been abducted…or worse."

God, I hope Maria's still alive.

"Damnation, Bringer, if one more spontaneous event crops up—"

Sanders reached over to snatch the USB drive from my

hand, and dialed her cell phone.

"This is Sanders. I need some agents to assist with a possible abduction at—," she ordered before stopping to glare at me. "Bringer, just where in the hell are we going?"

Despite my worry for Maria's welfare, I still could've kissed Sanders squarely on the lips at that moment.

CHAPTER 8

By the time we arrived at Maria's house, there were already local police cars and a sedan matching ours parked in front. Curious neighbors had started to gather as Sanders led the way past a patrol officer on the front porch.

Inside, I saw Maria's son and daughter nervously perched on the edge of the couch next to a man who I'd likely spoken on the phone to. At least, his voice seemed to match.

"...time that I arrived, the kids told me that they heard the doorbell ring as they were waking up. When they got up to look, they couldn't find their mother, so they immediately called me," the man recollected to a police sergeant and one of the FBI agents who I recognized from Sanders' office.

The guy noticed us enter and he stared at me.

"I'm Logan Bringer," I offered.

Then he pointed at me. "That's the guy that I told you about a few minutes ago."

I listened to Sanders and the other agent, but my attention kept being distracted by the sight of Maria's two children. No doubt, they wondered where their mother had gone so abruptly. I felt my frustration rise as the powerlessness of the situation registered on me. Worse yet, I had absolutely no idea where to start looking for her.

This just keeps getting worse and worse.

After nearly an hour of listening to questions and answers, I wandered into the kitchen just out of curiosity. I recalled that Maria had kept a shipment of my treatment formula in her refrigerator following the explosion at the Wallace Building. I opened the fridge, but instead of formula, I saw two pre-filled syringes in her cheese crisper and a small bottle of clear solution labeled, "LB Vitamins."

I heard the questions and answers still going on in the living room, so I slipped them into the interior pocket of my leather jacket.

I reasoned that the vitamin solution might be essential to continue boosting my brain's newfound capabilities. At least, given the dire circumstances, I was willing to use every edge that I could lay my hands on.

Before I returned to the living room, I walked over to the sink for a cup of cold water. When I returned to the other room, Sanders gave me a peculiar frown.

"Needed a swig of water," I said.

She rolled her eyes and squatted down next to the children to ask them questions in a low voice. Frankly, she looked quite at ease with Maria's children, just as she had with Agent Burroughs' daughters. I hadn't thought to ask her if she had children of her own.

Another hour passed, but by the time we left, we knew little more than when we'd arrived. As we sat in the car together traveling across town, I tried to determine the best way to inject myself with one of the syringes of vitamins that I'd taken from Maria's refrigerator.

I'd never been a fan of needles and never had a reason to bother with them, but the supplement was important and I needed every edge I could get for what may lay ahead.

"Where to now?" I asked.

"You do realize that you're not my partner in all this, right?" she asked.

"Fair enough," I said. "Then why don't you drop me off at my hotel and I'll be completely out of your hair."

She gave me a hard look.

"Not on your life," she emphatically stated. "You're right at the center of everything and I can't afford for *you* to disappear on me."

I shrugged.

"Besides, something tells me that you'll just go off like a loose cannon and end up getting into trouble or something," she added.

At that moment, I found it hard to disagree with her assessment.

* * *

Back at the office, her first act was to pick up her desk phone as she rotated the USB memory drive between her fingers.

"Hey, this is Sanders. I need for you to come by and pick up a memory drive. I want it scanned and then have the data uploaded to the network."

She paused.

"No, I haven't entered a helpdesk request," she said. "This is a matter of national security. Can't you cut me some slack?" she asked irritably.

She sighed.

"Fine. I'll enter the request and have it done by the time you get here. Just hurry," she said.

After she hung up, I suggested, "You do realize that you could just plug this into your computer. I'm fairly confident your computers must have adequate virus protection installed."

She appeared wholly annoyed by my observation.

"Yeah, well, they disabled the USB ports on all of our computers sometime last year."

"I could always burn it to CD for you," I suggested.

"They disabled our CD drives, too," she added. "Hell, I can't even get to Google mail to check my private emails anymore."

I stared at her with incredulity. Leave it to the government to render state-of-the-art technology perfectly useless. Typical government bureaucracy.

Never mind that you'd think FBI agents might *actually* need legitimate access to such technology to conduct their jobs effectively.

She sat down at her desk and frantically typed away at what must've been the bureaucratic helpdesk request.

"Are you certain these guys won't lose this drive?" I asked.

She looked up at me with an expression that might've chilled a volcano.

"Not exactly," she muttered with fallen features. "Actually, they did lose a data CD that I gave them about six months ago to upload. Oh, they finally found it, but not until almost a month later. We nearly botched an investigation without it."

"Ever hear of 'cleaning house?' " I asked.

"I wish, but we can't," she said. "About two years ago, the government's efficiency and budget streamlining committee approached the FBI. First, they laid off most of our office support staff. Then they let go of our in-house IT staff and hired a bunch of lowest-bidder civilian IT contractors who mostly punch a clock and collect a check. Can't fire them; can't threaten them. And we sure as hell can't motivate them to work faster. It takes about three times longer to get anything done, and it's rarely done correctly the first time around. And forget about it if you need help on weekends or holidays; their offices are unmanned."

I shook my head in disgust. "Ah, but think of all the money the government's saving."

"Yeah," she said with a sour expression. "Pretty soon, they'll outsource us agents."

That was a scary thought. Already I lived in a corporate-created city. What would happen when even the government itself became corporately outsourced?

"You know, after everything, there's still one thing that

the politicians and bureaucrats can't seem to either outsource or downsize," Sanders prompted.

I frowned. "Yeah? What's that?"

"The bureaucracy," she said.

I scowled. It reminded me of the military all over again.

"Sanders!" called Denton from the other side of the room. "My office. Now."

Agent Sanders groaned as she quickly made her way to her supervisor's office, pulling the glass door closed behind her as she entered.

I sat down in the guest chair at her desk and contemplated Maria's abduction. I tried not to think about what her circumstance was at that moment, including and especially her possible demise.

Then I thought about her children and the helpless, lost expressions on their faces.

Maria just had to be alive. And I had to find some way to locate her. Fast.

I felt a tingling sensation course through my head, which made me shiver. Then I started *hearing* bits and pieces of conversation.

No, it was more like thoughts; just as I'd experienced last night, like disembodied voices.

...that damned Bringer over to protective custody, someone thought.

He doesn't understand. Do I tell him everything? Would he even believe me, came Sanders' thought.

Raised voices emitted from Denton's closed office, and I noticed I wasn't the only person in the room who'd turned to look in that direction.

I quickly rose from my chair and walked directly to the office's glass door and knocked once before walking inside.

"What the hell are you doing in here?" Denton demanded. "I don't believe that anyone requested your presence."

Please don't do anything stupid, Sanders thought as she looked up at me wide-eyed.

What's this guy's problem, Denton thought.

"My problem is that you're not listening to your agent," I challenged.

"What?" Denton demanded.

How did he know---

"What you were thinking?" I finished his internal query.

Denton's mouth fell open.

"How in God's name did you just do that?" he asked.

What the hell, Sanders thought.

I tried to calm myself. Somehow, that seemed to allow me to pick up their thoughts easier.

"There's a lot about this case that you need to understand," I said. "Agent Sanders is your best chance of making heads or tails of this with me."

Denton stared at Sanders. "What is this guy, some sort of freak-show-mind reader? I thought you said Bringer was just some mild-mannered tag agency clerk or something."

"You said that?" I asked, staring down at Sanders.

She did a double-take at me, and stammered, "Well, sort of, but not exactly. I mean---"

"Never mind that," Denton cut her off before turning his full attention on me. "Okay, Mr. Mind Reader, what am I thinking?"

I felt my anxiety rise. It wasn't as if I fully understood how my abilities worked yet. Still, some things that Maria had told me seemed to be relatively accurate.

Maria.

I tried to force her from my mind and divert my full attention to Denton, who was staring at me with nearly bulging eyes.

"Go ahead, hot shot," he challenged.

I stared directly at him and tried to calm myself.

Pink flamingos, pink flamingos.

"Pink flamingos," I said.

His eyes widened momentarily, but then he frowned again.

"Beginner's luck," he said. "Try again, Bringer."

I stared at him and frowned. Somehow, I wasn't sensing anything.

"You're cheating. You're not thinking anything."

I hoped that I was actually correct and that my skill hadn't suddenly short-circuited.

He merely grunted.

"Again."

Oh, crap, Sanders thought. *I don't believe this.*

I glared at her. "Hey, how about a little more confidence here?"

She gawked at me.

This guy's a either a nutcase or he's the real deal, Denton thought. *How about 237 blueberry pies?*

I looked at him incredulously.

He scowled. "Gotcha', didn't I, Bringer?"

I crossed my arms and casually leaned against the doorjamb with a smug expression.

"Tell me something, Denton," I said. "Who in their right mind thinks about 237 blueberry pies?"

His expression immediately wilted.

"I'll be damned," he muttered. "Never in my life---"

"Oh, and Denton," I interrupted. "I'll admit that I'm trying my best to keep a lot of balls in the air all at once right now, and maybe I'm not the best at it. But I'm damn sure not a nutcase."

He appeared stunned. "Uh, yeah. Sorry about that."

Despite my bravado, I felt a wave of relief surge through me.

I'd actually done it!

Then I had to sit down because my legs suddenly felt like they were turning to Jell-O, and I half-fell into the spare guest chair before Denton's desk.

Crap.

"Are you okay?" Sanders asked.

"Yeah, I'm fine," I said. "But I think my blood sugar just tanked. I could use a Gatorade or something."

Both Sanders and Denton practically launched out of

their chairs.

* * *

By the time I'd finished consuming the sports drink that had been procured for me, Sanders had told Denton about everything she'd witnessed, including the bullets that had been intended for her on Friday night. In addition, I summarized information regarding my Nuclegene treatments and how my special abilities had developed as a result of my regimen.

"That explains the undamaged rounds we found on the front porch and in the back yard," Denton said as he stared at me. "Forensics has been baffled over that."

"We may want to leave them baffled a little while longer," Sanders suggested meaningfully.

"Who else knows about this?" he asked.

"You and I," Sanders replied.

"Burroughs knows, too," I offered.

"He does?" Sanders asked.

I nodded. "Yeah, we discussed it at the hospital after his surgery. Oh, and Maria Edwards knows. In fact, she's very important in multiple ways."

I explained how she had researched Nuclegene's databases, downloaded some of their records, and provided me key information about my treatments and condition, as well as helped me to understand my condition better.

"We need to find her," I urged. "The sooner the better. If for nothing else, there are two children who need their mother back."

"Agreed," Denton said.

Sanders nodded.

"I'll mobilize our team," Denton said. "But, Bringer, the best place for you is---"

"Out in the field with Agent Sanders," I interrupted. "Who else do you know who can read thoughts and potentially stop bullets as needed?"

Sanders appeared pleased at that.

Then I wondered if I'd actually be able to repeat those feats on demand.

"Yes, given the circumstances, I suppose that's been helpful. You've already saved one of my agent's lives," Denton said. "But you're also a principal in this case. You're not even in law enforcement; you're just a civilian."

"Actually, I'm more of a consultant," I challenged.

"Hardly. You're a witness at the very least, though obviously a lot more," he countered.

"Then I'm under the protective custody of Agent Sanders," I said.

Denton appeared introspective.

"Agreed," Sanders spoke up.

Denton sighed. "I could lose my ass over this."

I nodded. "Yeah, or you could break one of the highest-profile cases in the country, and maybe save a mother's life."

Denton scowled. "True, I suppose."

"However, there's one more thing," I said.

"Yeah?"

"The fire at my sister's was no accident," I said.

I explained the phone call that I'd received in conjunction with the timing of the fire.

"My family needs protection until this is resolved."

Denton nodded. "I understand. I'll see what I can do. At the very least, we should be able to temporarily enlist the help of local police for additional protection," he said. "In the meantime, you don't do *anything* without running it through Sanders first. She takes the lead. I'm not turning you loose on some sort of personal agenda. Got it?"

Sanders appeared quite pleased with herself.

But Denton turned his attention to Sanders and pointed his finger at her.

"And *you*, keep his ass alive. I don't want any heroics, special abilities or not. We do this as a team, got it?"

"Yes, sir," she replied. "By the book."

Denton drew in a deep breath and ran his fingers

through his hair. "Yeah, well, I think we're already operating in the gray on this case. At the very least, I'm getting really creative with the rules."

"Sounds fine to me," I said. "Now, how about a visitor's badge?"

This guy's a real comedian, Denton thought.

I tapped my temple with one fingertip. "I heard that."

CHAPTER 9

Maria Edwards.

I was obsessed with finding her. And the quicker that we did, the better her chances were of being found alive. Fortunately, Agent Sanders shared both my concern and growing sense of urgency.

The foremost problem? Where to start.

Given that Maria was employed by the Nuclegene Corporation, Sanders determined that our first destination was the company's local offices, located in the prestigious thirty-story Hamilton Financial Tower downtown. The towering structure was located amidst a two-block square area of prime real estate; the center of corporate powers within the city. A number of the highest-profile financial companies and businesses maintained offices in the Hamilton building.

As we waited for an elevator to take us up to the twelfth floor, Sanders prompted, "Let me do the talking. Just listen in for anything useful."

"Got it," I replied, eyeing my khaki slacks and golf shirt and then glancing at her charcoal grey pantsuit.

"You look fine," she assured me. "And, Bringer?"

I stared into her hazel eyes.

"Stay out of my head," she warned.

I winked at her as the doors opened to reveal a

professionally decorated entry area for Nuclegene Corporation's local offices. The company had secured two floors of the exclusive building, which seemed considerable given the powerful competing interests sharing square footage in the tower.

After Sanders flashed her credentials, she repeated the whole "we're with the FBI" routine, which came off as rather impressive, given that I wasn't on the receiving end of it.

"I'll just ring Mr. Feinstein's office for you," said the receptionist.

"Mr. Feinstein?" Sanders asked.

"Yes, Mr. Feinstein is Director of our Nevis Corners offices."

Moments later, an administrative assistant quickly escorted us to a nearby spacious office that appeared nondescript, most apparent by the lack of visible personal effects amidst the small stacks of paperwork and folders. However, a nameplate was slightly askew at the front of the desk with the name Max Feinstein inscribed.

"Someone will be with you shortly," the administrative assistant said, and then quickly extricated herself from the room.

I looked at Sanders with a curious expression but she merely shrugged.

A lady dressed impeccably in a crisp-looking business suit stepped into the office.

"Good afternoon," she greeted. "I'm Betty Haskins, Director of Personnel Services. How can I assist you?"

"We're here to meet with the local director or administrator. Would that be Max Feinstein?"

"I'm afraid that won't be possible as Mr. Feinstein is no longer with the company," Betty Haskins said.

"Since?"

"Earlier today, in fact," she said.

Sanders and I exchanged curious glances.

"Then who's in charge here?" Sanders pressed.

The woman's former confident-looking composure

faltered slightly, so I closed my eyes and tried to clear my thoughts.

"I'll have to inquire further," Haskins said.

...*runaround from these people*, Sanders projected.

...*asked that we not refer anyone to Mr. Bernard*, thought Haskins.

Guy's gotta cute butt, came a passing woman's thoughts.

I opened my eyes and turned to gaze at the curvaceous brunette who looked in at us as she passed by the open doorway. When I turned back to look at Sanders, she glared at me before turning to Ms. Haskins.

"No need. We'll speak with Mr. Bernard then," I interjected.

That seemed to catch the director off guard, and she stammered, "I see. Well, I'll have to check first."

Minutes later, we stood before another desk that was part of a far more elaborate wing of the floor. Everything surrounding us screamed money.

However, it struck me as peculiar that the entire area seemed new, as if recently remodeled. I also noticed a fellow in a crisp business suit following behind us as soon as we entered the area. His bearing hinted at a military background.

The lady at the desk before us, Sandra Yalesin, was a petite woman with long blonde hair and blue eyes. Yet, she carried herself with the air of someone who bore some authority; evidently somewhat higher in the pecking order than Ms. Haskins.

I focused on clearing my thoughts as much as possible.

"Mr. Bernard is a very busy man, I'm afraid," Ms. Yalesin hedged. "Perhaps I could arrange an appointment for him to meet with you another time?"

Before Sanders could reply, I said flatly, "Please tell him that Logan Bringer is also here to meet with him."

Now, what's he up to, Sanders thoughts passed across my heightened awareness.

The woman's eyebrows arched slightly.

"And are you acquainted with Mr. Bernard?"

"Not as such, but he'll likely still want to see me," I replied.

I was playing poker on a whim, hoping that Maria's corporate conspiracy theory was prevalent upward through Nuclegene's leadership.

An intercom abruptly activated.

"Ms. Yalesin, please invite our visitors in, won't you?"

"Yes, sir," she replied.

The silent fellow who'd been shadowing us opened the large oak door leading into an expansive corner office with two glass walls looking out onto the city. A tall, barrel-chested fifty-something-looking man with graying hair walked around an oversized desk to greet us. He sported a dark suit that must've had a better thread count than most any Arabian prince had in his closet.

"Welcome, Agent Sanders and Mr. Bringer," he offered with an outstretched hand. "I'm Clive Bernard, President of Nuclegene Corporation."

As we shook hands with Bernard, the quiet man who'd been following us closed the door behind us and stood at semi-attention.

"It's a pleasure to meet both of you, but particularly you, Mr. Bringer. I believe you're one of our company's most recent cancer success stories," Bernard said.

...is why Bringer would be here, came a stray thought from him.

"I hope so," I replied.

"Yet, such a horrible tragedy about our Wallace Building center; all those wonderful staff and patients," Bernard added. "I hope the FBI brings good news of progress."

"As a matter of fact, we're here concerning the investigation," Sanders said.

"Please, have a seat," Bernard gestured to a set of regal-looking leather chairs before his desk. "May I get you something to drink? Coffee, perhaps?"

"Thank you, no," Sanders replied. "For the record, Mr. Bernard, are you the chief authority within Nuclegene

Corporation?"

Bernard sat in an oversized leather chair behind his desk that threatened to engulf the man. I opened my thoughts and waited to listen in on anything useful.

She's very direct, came a stray thought.

"Essentially, I'm the company's head of operations," he replied. "However, Nevis Wallace, the company's founder and chairman of the Board of Directors, remains in hierarchical control of the company."

"So, Mr. Wallace would essentially be the Chief Executive Officer, which means that you work directly for him," Sanders speculated.

"Precisely," said Bernard. "Although Mr. Wallace rarely presides over the company's day-to-day operations."

"Isn't it unusual for the company's president to be presiding here when your corporate headquarters are based in New York?" Sanders asked.

"I temporarily relocated here due to the Wallace Building disaster in order to preside over corporate affairs and the rebuilding effort," he said. "It was at the request of Mr. Wallace, you see. Many are unaware that, as one of the Nevis Corners' principal founders and city namesakes, Mr. Wallace has more than a passing interest in what takes place here."

Too close to home this time, I silently eavesdropped.

"Do you know Ms. Maria Edwards?" Sanders asked.

I should've anticipated that," Bernard thought.

"Yes. Ms. Edwards is a physician's assistant who formerly worked in the Wallace Building," he replied. "I believe the poor woman has gone missing, according to a news report I saw this morning."

...still waiting on our team to report back, came another fleeting thought.

I honed in on Bernard's thoughts, hoping to glean as much information as possible about Maria.

"Do you know anything concerning Maria's whereabouts, Mr. Bernard?" Sanders asked.

"No," he smoothly replied. "Although I wish I did, for

her sake."

...*Continuance Corporation outmaneuvering us*, he thought.

"Really nice office, Mr. Bernard," I said. "Too nice for a local administrator. Mr. Feinstein's wasn't nearly so nice, I noticed. Yours is much more presidential-looking. Are you considering relocating your corporate headquarters here on a more permanent basis?"

Sanders frowned at me with a look of stark disapproval. However, Mr. Bernard seemed momentarily unsettled by my question.

What does he know? Bernard projected.

"Although this topic isn't currently public, I'll confide to you that the company is preparing to undergo some restructuring," he replied. "Quite naturally, companies reorganize from time to time, which occasionally involves relocation of assets or changes in staffing."

"Like Max Feinstein?" Sanders asked.

"Precisely," Bernard said.

"Have you chatted with anyone recently about a reduction in staff? Say, perhaps, a tall fellow with red hair," I asked.

Dammit, Bringer, Sanders projected.

Bernard's face turned to stone.

...*maybe not the FBI after all*, came a gruff voice in my head.

I flew out of my chair just as the man behind us started moving forward. I half-imagined punching him, even as my fist was propelling forward, and he flew back against the wall with a thud.

My fist never even impacted him!

His right hand snaked inside his suit coat under his left arm as Sanders kicked her chair aside and drew her pistol in one smooth movement.

"Freeze!" she commanded, her pistol pointed directly at him.

"Wait!" Bernard ordered, still seated behind the desk. "Scott, these aren't the enemy."

Bringer's abilities manifested, came a stray thought.

"Slowly remove your weapon and place it on the floor," Sanders ordered. "Now, move slowly to stand behind your boss with your hands where I can see them."

Sanders remained standing with her weapon trained.

"Bernard, you'd better give me a damn good reason why I don't arrest you both for attempted assault and obstruction."

Wow, what a fireball of a lady.

She looked over at me and frowned. "You okay?"

I quickly wiped the smirk from my face.

"Agent Sanders, events are transpiring behind the scenes that are well beyond the destruction of a building, dozens of innocent deaths, or a missing employee," Bernard calmly stated as he slowly folded his hands on the desktop before him. "Frankly, an agency like the FBI is in way over its head here."

"Go on," Sanders prompted.

"Governments rise and fall, politicians come and go, but in the past two centuries, corporations continue to thrive," Bernard continued. "The struggle between such entities reshapes not only the business landscape, but the development of the world's cultures and societies."

Great, this guy turned all Gordon Gecko on us all of the sudden. Even his thoughts mirrored his words.

Concentrating only on his speech for the time being, I righted our chairs. Sanders perched on the edge of hers with her pistol balanced in one hand.

"And your point is?" she pressed.

"You're not investigating a terrorist act, or a kidnapping," Bernard said. "You've delved into the middle of nothing short of a small, clandestine corporate war."

Something Bernard had thought about earlier popped into my head, so I played a hunch.

"Mr. Bernard, talk to us about Continuance Corporation," I prompted. "And don't worry; I think you'll find I'm pretty good with wars."

Admittedly, an understatement.

Wars of foreign religions and ideologies, as well as disease. Wars in my head that I'd only begun to reconcile.

I'd already had my fill of both Islamic militants and cancer. Fortunately, I'd survived both.

So far.

Sanders spared me a look of approval that was nothing short of spectacular.

"I'm intrigued to know what you've heard about Continuance Corporation, Mr. Bringer," he replied.

I inclined my head in acknowledgement. "I'm sure you are. However, I think what you have to say would be much more enlightening."

"Very well," he said. "Continuance Corporation, or Bestand Gesellschaft as it was known in Germany when it was founded in 1953, was born during the early days of the Cold War in collaboration between the U.S. government, medical researchers, and powerful businessmen with interests in the paranormal.

"However, their ventures were often fruitless, and in 1977 the U.S. government severed its ties with, and subsequent interest in, the company. By 1982, Continuance Corporation had teetered into complete bankruptcy."

"What does Continuance have to do with your company, Mr. Bernard?"

"An excellent question, Agent Sanders," he replied with a nod. "Actually, everything. We are Continuance Corporation's primary worldwide competition."

I noticed Sanders was frowning. I wondered why until I replayed what Bernard just said. Then it hit me.

"Wait. You just said Continuance went bankrupt in 1982," I said.

"Officially, the company did," Bernard replied. "However, that hardly means they ceased operations."

"I'm a little confused," Sanders interjected. "How does a bankrupt corporation manage to successfully continue operations? Receivership?"

Bernard's features hardened. "The company went underground, actually. They're not listed on any international stock exchange, nor have they filed any operational documents with any nation since 1982."

"Then how do they compete with Nuclegene?" I asked.

"They steal our research, sabotage our operations, and counter-develop our innovations for sale on the black market, of course," Bernard said as if he were explaining to children why the grass was green.

Sanders remained silent but I could almost see the wheels turning in her head. My own mental wheels were turning, as well.

"Continuance blew up the Wallace Building just to sabotage Nuclegene's operations. More to the point, they sabotaged your company's latest development," I said.

Except for me.

It was a rather cold epiphany on my part.

"Precisely," Bernard replied.

"Why didn't you come forward to the authorities with this already, Mr. Bernard?" Sanders demanded.

"Because it's not as if the U.S. government would be of any great assistance. Do you believe they could track down a shadow company? How do you expect them to freeze assets or shut down operations of an organization that doesn't officially exist?" Bernard explained.

He had a point.

"Rather, you wouldn't want to release information about your company's interests in research that isn't sanctioned by the FDA," Sanders suggested. "More to the point, you'd probably hate to acknowledge the successful achievement of your research until it could be properly marketed."

Bernard's expression appeared pleasant yet cool; much like a practiced chess player who'd reluctantly conceded a match.

"You're a very perceptive investigator, Agent Sanders," he offered. "And as has just been displayed, it would seem that our research has resulted in a successful development."

Sanders alternated looking between Bernard and me with an expression of incredulity.

"Do you mean that Nuclegene Corporation is developing a drug to create paranormal abilities in humans?" she asked incredulously.

"What you're referring to is *psychic* abilities," Bernard corrected her. "Instead, our company is focused on empathic and telekinetic abilities. We're not dealing in vampires, werewolves, ghosts, or magic here, Agent Sanders."

I noticed Sanders' jaw clench.

"If this is such a secret, why are you telling us this now?" she asked coolly.

Bernard gave a rueful sigh. "Alas, the benefits currently outweigh the risk. Now that I've confirmed Mr. Bringer's abilities, I'm afraid I'm going to need to ask for your, and his, assistance. And I do hope that I can secure your discretion in these matters."

Sanders and I exchanged curious expressions.

"You do realize that I work for the FBI, Mr. Bernard," Sanders clarified. "I'm not for hire, and I have an obligation to report any developments related to this case."

"That's your purview, Agent Sanders. I'm merely asking that you continue your investigations, and hopefully locate who's behind the destruction of our facilities and death of our employees and patients, as well as the disappearance of Ms. Edwards," Bernard equivocated.

"But you'd like for me to leave out the part about Nuclegene's sensitive research," Sanders baited. "I'm afraid that's not entirely possible."

"Naturally," he agreed with a shrug. "However, you should carefully consider what you share. You may find there are those within our own government who may have a mutual interest in curtailing that same information, no matter how well-intended or duty bound you consider yourself to be."

Bernard alluded to something else dark and disturbing.

Were some government officials already aware of what's

going on?

Although it wouldn't have surprised me in the least if a cover-up might already be in the works. I'd been in the Army, after all, and I recognized how seemingly overt events could suddenly be declared clandestine.

"And what about you, Mr. Bringer?" Bernard asked.

"Right now, my primary concern is finding Maria Edwards," I replied evenly. "And I don't give a damn who gets in my way."

"Admirable," Bernard replied. "Not that I disagree with you in the least, please understand."

"Mr. Bernard, I suggest you turn over any additional information that you have at your disposal that might be related to this case," Sanders said.

"As a matter of fact, I do have some things that may prove helpful," he said.

Bernard reached over to his phone and activated the intercom.

"Ms. Yalesin, would you please bring me a copy of the list of names that we discussed earlier this morning?"

"Of course, Mr. Bernard," Yalesin crisply replied.

* * *

By the time we left Nuclegene's offices, though notably sans any arrestees, we at least had a list of names to investigate. Bernard thought any one of them might be related to our investigation, as they were individuals that his own intelligence assets had associated with Continuance Corporation operations.

Hell, it seemed as if we were tracking a terrorist group rather than some underground corporation.

"Nice work back there," Sanders complimented as she drove us back to the FBI office.

"Thanks," I replied. "But tell me something; why is Bernard still sitting up in his office instead of accompanying us to your office?"

"Admittedly, it's against my better judgment. But something told me that someone in Bernard's position wouldn't be in custody long enough for us to ask any questions," she replied. "At least he's not openly hostile with us, and that's something helpful."

I rubbed my temples with my fingertips. One of my throbbing headaches was coming on. I suppose I'd already expended some efforts with my abilities that morning.

Telekinetic abilities, no less.

It sounded surreal to put a name like that to what I could do.

"Does your head always hurt after you use your abilities?" Sanders asked.

I nodded, which didn't help the growing throbbing.

"Yeah, but it usually goes away when I hydrate," I said.

She looked over at me with a concerned expression.

A few minutes later, she pulled in front of a nearby convenience store.

"Fuel up," she said good-naturedly.

I felt a lot better once I'd consumed about a third of a bottle of sports drink.

CHAPTER 10

"This changes the dynamic of the investigation considerably," Chuck Denton said once Sanders and I had briefed him on our visit with Bernard at the Nuclegene offices.

"How so? It hardly changes our overall goal," I challenged.

"No," Denton replied. "But it means that we to keep an even tighter lid on all information, just in case Bernard's correct about competing interests from within our government. Speaking of which, the guys in IT finished downloading the documents from the memory drive that you provided. Sanders, they're in a folder on the network that only our team has access to."

"And the private contractor IT support staff who gave you access to it," I added dryly.

Denton frowned at me. "Yeah. I'll try not to dwell too much on that."

"I'll run these names through our database and see if I can get a hit on any of them," Sanders said.

"Good," Denton said as we rose to leave his office. "Keep me in the loop."

He rose and handed me a small sheet of paper and a plastic badge.

"What's this?" I asked.

"The VIP badge will get you into the building and our office area. The paper has the names of our team members, including their office and cell phone numbers. Put those in your phone and wallet, and please don't share them with anyone. I've already provided the team with your contact information."

"Thanks."

It felt good to be part of something useful again. I just wished the circumstances were better.

"Welcome to our team," he offered with a quick handshake. "Although you may find that you've signed on for more than you expected. Just remember, you're not on the payroll, and there may be a few circumstances where even being under FBI protective custody might not shield you from scrutiny."

"I'll remember that."

"Now, follow Sanders and get to work."

I nodded and we returned to Sanders' desk while I mulled over what Denton had just said. It made me wonder what sort of *circumstances* he meant.

To my surprise, Sanders logged into the FBI's information database and showed me how to conduct simple searches. Then she asked me to perform a search on all of the names on the list that Bernard had given us.

"But don't let anyone else except agents in our office see you on my workstation, okay? If anybody asks me, I don't know anything about it," she warned before leaving to do some additional information gathering.

I scowled.

Plausible deniability. Gotta' love it.

To my surprise, the computer searches yielded only two hits, though neither individual had any priors. With the assistance of a cute blonde-haired, blue-eyed agent named Lana Collins, I was able to access their last known addresses. A young lady named Justine Ziska was listed in New York City, and a guy named Thomas Gibbons had a Chicago,

Illinois address.

Sanders alerted FBI offices in both cities and made hasty arrangements for us to catch the next flight to Chicago. The New York office would initiate surveillance on Justine Ziska.

Fortunately, Sanders received word that I'd regained use of my home, so we hastily dropped by my place on the way to the airport. At least I'd be able to change into some dress pants and shirt so that I could blend in next to Sanders somewhat authentically.

"You're actually not hard on the eyes when you're presentably dressed, Bringer," she quipped with an appraising expression.

I flashed a charming grin at her, but she merely rolled her eyes. However, the moment quickly faded as my thoughts returned to Maria Edwards.

In actuality, it was a relatively short flight to Chicago but it felt like forever given the urgent nature of our trip. Flight time aside, O'Hare International Airport was something entirely different.

For a guy like me who had done very little traveling in recent years, it felt like a madhouse; barely controlled chaos teeming with people. However, I quietly admired the seamless manner that Sanders negotiated a host of harried airport experiences; chiefly, passenger screening and boarding. Of course, having the full influence of the FBI behind us hadn't hurt, either.

We were met by two agents from the Chicago office, Buddy Cross and Peter Harker; both of whom sported the textbook dark suits and neatly trimmed haircuts. Both men cordially greeted Agent Sanders, but turned decidedly more guarded when I introduced myself. I couldn't help wondering if my newfound abilities weren't somehow subliminally influencing people.

Then again, maybe I was just being paranoid.

"Mr. Bringer's of paramount importance to our investigation and is under the agency's protection," Sanders explained.

Both men eyed me dubiously before leading us through the airport toward the parking garage. I tried to open my mind in an attempt to read their thoughts, but I was assailed by a din of voices that nearly brought me to a halt mid-step. I quickly shut my mind off again, even before realizing that I'd done it.

"You okay?" Sanders whispered as we approached the Ford sedan in the parking garage.

"Yeah, sure," I said.

Hell, the truth was, I hadn't felt *okay* in what seemed liked ages. Maybe managing to find Maria and safely returning her to her kids might help with that.

"Chicago PD is assisting us on this," Agent Cross explained from the front passenger seat. "They're positioned a reasonable distance from the address you gave us. Plus, we've got a couple of other agents already on scene. Our field supervisor, Kip Desmond, is meeting us there."

Despite the heavy traffic, we seemed to make it to the west side of town relatively quickly. The part of the city we found ourselves in appeared to be in decline, and a number of unsavory-looking characters glared at us as we passed by. I tried to focus my thoughts on my abilities, gently probing at my skills just in case they were needed.

I made the spare seatbelt between Sanders and me float up from the seat cushion a few inches. She did a double-take at the display and then slapped her hand on top of it while giving me a hard look, shaking her head negatively.

I innocently shrugged as our car came to a halt in the small parking lot of a neighborhood grocery store. As we stepped from the vehicle, the rear door to a nearby unmarked panel van opened to reveal a group of people, including a police officer wearing SWAT gear and a business suit-clad man and woman.

"Agents Kip Desmond and Sally Brinks," Cross introduced. "This is Agent Sanders and Mr. Bringer from the Nevis Corners office."

Following a brief series of handshakes, everyone busied

themselves with preparations. The agents were each fitted with earpieces and microphones that appeared like the ones often depicted in the movies for Secret Service agents.

In truth, the entire situation felt a little like a movie set, except that Maria's life was in very real danger.

I followed Agents Cross and Sanders as we walked less than a block to the unkempt-looking five-story apartment building that was listed as Thomas Gibbons' last-known address. We located the apartment manager, a middle-aged and balding man named Tippins, who agreed to let us into Gibbons' apartment, though not before Cross showed him a newly-acquired search warrant.

Again, just like in the movies.

"Do you know if Mr. Gibbons is here right now, Mr. Tippins?" Sanders asked as we exited the elevator on the third floor.

"I really can't say," Tippins replied. "Honestly, I just collect the rent and try to keep everything in semi-working order around here."

The sounds from a blaring television, a crying baby, and loud music culminated in the hallway from different apartments. Cross and Sanders removed their pistols from their holsters and held them in guarded positions.

I tried to open my thoughts, and was assailed by a host of disembodied voices.

...hope the guy doesn't have a dead body up here, Tippins thought.

...ready for anything, Cross thought.

...stop crying for God's sake, a woman thought.

...hope he's here, Sanders thought.

Sanders signaled for Tippins and me to stand behind her as she and Cross stood on either side of the door to apartment 305.

Cross knocked on the wooden door.

"Mr. Gibbons? FBI," Cross said. "We have a warrant to search your premises. Please open the door."

There was no response and I wasn't sensing any

thoughts from inside. I gently tapped Sanders on the elbow and she looked back at me in silent query.

I pointed to my head and shook my head in negative fashion.

"Open it," she ordered Tippins.

The apartment was unoccupied, but had quite evidently been lived in. Fortunately, there were no dead bodies inside, specifically Maria's.

After being cautioned not to touch anything, I looked around for anything of interest that was lying about. A dated-looking photo of a twenty-something looking man standing next to an older lady was on a living room shelf.

I wondered if it was Gibbons and a relative; perhaps his mother or aunt.

Agents Harker, Brinks, and Desmond collaborated with a police forensics team, which quickly filled the small apartment. I wandered out into the main hallway where a lone, bored-looking police officer stood outside the apartment.

I heard a door open at the end of the hallway and turned to gaze into an astonished-looking man's face. He appeared to be about ten years older than the man who I'd just seen in the photo.

It had to be Gibbons.

The man darted back from where he came, and I yelled, "Gibbons!"

I took off down the hallway with the Chicago police officer trailing at my heels. By the time I hit the door leading into the stairwell, I caught a sidelong glimpse of Sanders and Harker heading in our direction.

"He's in the stairwell!" Sanders yelled. "Cover all the exits and search floor by floor!"

I made it to the second floor landing but still heard footsteps ahead of me, so I kept going. The young police officer and I hurried neck-in-neck down the stairs.

Then the young officer slipped and fell forward ahead of me. I lunged to reach out for him but caught only a handful of air.

"Shit!" he yelled.

Fortunately, my mind was faster, and I practically *sensed* a large weight before me. I jerked my hand backward and his body fell back against the concrete steps with a thud.

"Thanks!" I heard him shout as I rushed downstairs.

I heard a door open and slam shut seconds before I made it to the bottom floor, only to be confronted with two doors. I started to barrel through the door labeled *Lobby*, but paused and opened my mind.

...*somebody over to the alley right now.*

...*get him if he hits the lobby*, came another person's thoughts.

I changed direction and barreled through the other door, only belatedly realizing what a bad idea that might be. However, rather than an ambush, I saw Gibbons fleeing at the end of the alleyway.

I knew I'd never catch him, so I concentrated on a metal trash dumpster just ahead of where he was running. Half-sensing something substantial, I imagined grasping the structure and jerked my hand back toward me.

The dumpster slammed into the man with a force that knocked him back into the alley. Then a heavy pain roared through my head that was so intense it dropped me to my knees.

A bout of nausea assailed me as I struggled to rise to my feet.

I couldn't afford to lose that guy. We were already grasping at straws as it was.

I willed myself to put each foot before me, racing to reach Gibbons, who was struggling to rise from his prone position on the ground.

As I reached him, he'd just regained his footing and was staggering forward, appearing slightly stunned. I grabbed him by the shirt and propelled him against the nearby garbage bin.

"Where's Maria Edwards?" I demanded. "Tell me!"

He stared back at me with a wide-eyed expression. I tried

to open my mind to his thoughts but was having trouble focusing as I held him against the container. Then I heard rapid footsteps coming up the alleyway toward us.

...Wenzel.

"Freeze!" yelled someone nearby.

I slammed Gibbons against the bin again, and demanded, "Wenzel, who?!"

He stared at me as if I was some kind of monster.

"Bringer, let him go!" Agent Sanders insisted as she pried at my right arm.

...can't tell him about Hadrian, the man thought.

A set of hands gripped my other arm, and Agent Harker ordered, "We've got him. Let him go!"

I released Gibbons as Sanders and Harker cuffed him and read him his Miranda rights. Meanwhile, I strained to glean what I could from the man's thoughts.

Unfortunately, there was too much mental noise surrounding me, like too many people talking at once.

Who the hell does that guy think he is?

...going to get into trouble, Bringer.

...they'll kill me. Gibbons thought trickled through.

More police officers, including Agents Cross and Desmond, arrived to add to the mental commotion, so I shut down my ability just to keep from drowning in disjointed voices. It was then I realized that I was consciously channeling my skills somewhat effectively.

"Who's Wenzel? Who's Hadrian?" I demanded of Gibbons as Harker took hold of the cuffed man's arm to lead him back down the alleyway.

Gibbons merely stared back at me like I was Satan incarnate.

"Not saying anything," he muttered.

At that moment, I'd have liked to try to beat it out of him.

"Did he tell you something?" Agent Desmond asked.

I shrugged while rubbing at my temples with my fingertips. My head hurt like hell.

"Not in so many words," I muttered.

"Um, we've been following up on a lot of disjointed leads on this case," Sanders neatly interjected as she scribbled something onto a small notepad.

Desmond grunted, but Agent Cross looked at me with a peculiar expression.

"Good thing you caught him," Cross ventured. "He had a pretty good start on you, didn't he?"

"Bringer's ex-army," Sanders said. "He's in pretty good shape, actually."

I looked at her with a semi-amused expression but she pointedly ignored me. However, Desmond chuckled.

"Well, lucky for us the guy ran headfirst into this trash dumpster, too," I said.

"Yeah," Cross said in a dubious tone. "Damned lucky."

At the front of the apartment building, the agents loaded Gibbons into the back seat of one of the police cars. Agent Harker accompanied him.

"I want two officers in Gibbons' car," Desmond ordered, to which a police sergeant nodded.

"I'd like to accompany Gibbons, as well," Sanders said.

"Nothing to worry about. We'll interrogate Gibbons downtown once they process him," Desmond said. "Sanders, you and Bringer can ride with Cross and me. We'll follow them in together. Agent Brinks is going to stay onsite with the forensics team."

Minutes later, I sat in the back seat of a sedan with Sanders as we followed the police car through the city.

Sanders gently nudged me with her elbow. "You okay?" she whispered.

I nodded. Fortunately, the achiness in my head had subsided somewhat. The truth was, I would've given most anything for a Gatorade at that moment. I noticed Cross staring back at me with a suspicious expression in the rear view mirror as he drove.

"You think this guy has something to do with the Wallace Building explosion?" Desmond asked.

"Possibly," Sanders replied.

"What the hell?" Cross asked as he stared ahead.

Sanders and I simultaneously sat forward to look out through the windshield. The lead police car transporting Gibbons swerved erratically as it approached the next major intersection and then slammed into an oncoming vehicle.

"Jesus!" Desmond exclaimed.

Agent Cross initiated the siren on our car while swerving out of the way of an oncoming vehicle that had cascaded into our lane.

"Shit!" Cross cursed.

Our car came to a halt less than twenty feet from the crashed police car ahead of us. Its front hood was crumpled and smoke was pouring out from the hood.

I glanced to my left just in time to see an oncoming full-size Hummer bearing directly at us.

"Hold on!" I yelled.

The Hummer impacted the driver's side of our vehicle full-on, displacing our vehicle and propelling me against Sanders to my right. The front airbags immediately deployed, knocking Cross and Desmond back into their seats.

Half-dazed, I heard shouts and horns, as well as the warbling of our car's siren around me.

Sanders moaned and I struggled to sit up.

Then I heard gunshots.

Sanders managed to unholster her weapon as she opened her car door and the two of us half-fell onto the street outside. I looked inside and noticed that Cross was unconscious or worse, as well as partially pinned behind the steering wheel. Desmond appeared only half-aware of his surroundings as he popped his passenger door open and attempted to draw his own weapon.

I looked beyond the hood of our car toward the crashed police car and saw a red-haired man standing beside the vehicle. Using an assault rifle, he rapid-fired into the vehicle less than twenty yards from us.

It was the guy who'd tried to kill Sanders and myself.

"It's him!" I yelled.

Sanders aimed her pistol at the man and shouted, "Freeze! FBI!"

The man pivoted toward us and his rifle belched with flame. I heard rounds impact the vehicle around us, and I managed to grab Sanders' jacket to pull her down to the pavement with me. I noticed that she had a bleeding cut on her forehead.

I realized our hopes of interrogating Gibbons were all but lost if we didn't stop that red-haired bastard. I jumped up from behind the side of the car, even as Sanders grabbed at my jacket.

"Don't!" she shouted.

I was so pissed that I barely heard her. Instead, I focused on the rifle-wielding man before me and held out my hand. With every fiber of my being, I reached out with my talent and pushed. The man flew backward against the car as if he'd been thrown against it. Immediately, pain shot through my head.

Sanders stood up from behind the cover of our car and aimed her pistol, even as the man recovered, pointing his weapon downrange at us.

I held up my hand in a shielding fashion and felt a hammering in my head that was ten-fold what I'd felt on the two prior occasions. The pain almost overwhelmed me.

Through watering eyes, I saw, as well as felt, the small objects suspended before me. I heard Sanders' weapon firing behind me, and watched the red-haired man twitch from the impacts before falling to his knees and doubling over.

I let my talent ebb and heard the dull sounds of small metallic objects clanking before us against the pavement. Sanders edged past me with her weapon held before her as she tactically approached the prone man.

Less than ten feet from him, he rose up with a pistol in his hand and pointed it at Sanders.

"NO!" I shouted, initiating my talent.

The man flew up over the police car and into the air,

even as I half-blacked out from the pain in my head. I heard two shots, but couldn't tell where they came from. Then I heard a heavy sounding thud, followed by the wail of sirens and screaming from all around me.

I vaguely realized that I was on my hands and knees trying to crawl toward Sanders, still unable to see very well through the foggy half-darkness threatening to overcome me.

I felt small hands grabbing at my shoulders, and then Sanders' urgent voice say, "Bringer! Are you hit, Logan?"

"Thank God you're okay," I half-choked. "What about Gibbons?"

"They're all dead," Sanders lamented. "We didn't stop him in time."

I felt a sense of time displacement as I sat down on the asphalt beneath me, struggling to refocus my vision. The attempt initiated a surge of pain in my head.

"Just sit there," Sanders insisted. "I'll be back."

The sheer helplessness I felt wasn't only infuriating, it felt humiliating. Admittedly, I was in no position to do anything more.

By the time my head began to clear and my vision had fully returned, Agent Desmond was barking orders to other police officers in the area. Agent Sanders showed up with some variety of soda, which I gratefully took from her. I downed it in less than a minute, and felt a series of tingling sensations permeating through my body.

My electrolytes were being replenished.

"Where's the gunman?" I asked a nearby police officer.

He appeared completely puzzled. "Dunno. We haven't found him yet."

Where the hell had he gone after I launched him airborne?

Within the hour, Sanders and I sat in an oversized office down at the local FBI office in downtown Chicago. I noticed that she had a small bandage on her forehead.

A perplexed-looking woman in business attire plopped a small jug of Gatorade onto the table next to me and then left the room. Sanders stared at me as I unscrewed the lid and took a big swig of the cold contents.

"Feeling any better?" she asked with concern.

"No," I grunted. "What happened to that damned gunman out there?"

Sanders appeared momentarily speechless before replying, "I honestly don't know. I remember thinking that I was going to die, and then he just 'flew' into the air and disappeared. I *know* that I saw his body land on the street some thirty feet away from us. Then, I looked down at you and when I glanced back a moment later, he was gone."

"I can't believe that," I said. "Nobody should be able to just walk away from that. Hell, you even shot him, for Christ's sake."

Sanders shook her head. "At least, I thought so. He must've been wearing body armor of some kind."

We sat in silence for a few minutes.

"Two officers and Agent Harker are all dead. Our best lead is dead, too," Sanders said acidly. "And Agent Cross is in the hospital, I'm told. This whole investigation is a complete cluster fuck!"

I stopped mid-drink to stare over at her with surprise. It was the first time I'd heard Sanders use that tone or language.

"Hey, just how many times have you had a case like this?" I challenged. "I'm seeing shit happen out there that shouldn't even be able to happen. I've been in friggin' war zones where shit like that doesn't even happen."

Sanders stared back at me with a blank expression.

"Yeah, well, I suppose we'd be dead, too, if your *shit* hadn't happened when it did," she said with resignation.

I had no response for that.

Agents Desmond and Brinks walked into the office and wearily sunk into chairs next to us. Both had tired, half-shocked expressions on their faces.

I'd definitely seen those expressions before in another time and place.

"I can't properly put this day into words," Desmond began. "We've lost a fellow agent, in addition to the other lives lost. And I've got a wounded gunman running around the streets of Chicago somewhere. Not to mention, I saw something that defies not only logic, but sanity. I've also got witnesses saying that a man was mysteriously catapulted into the air today."

Desmond's gaze bore into me like a man possessed.

"Look, I can't even begin to fully understand what you two are in the middle of," he continued. "So you'll pardon me for asking, but what in *God's name* managed to launch that gunman into the air today? And just how did you do it?"

"I'm afraid that we can't speak to that in any detail at this time, Agent Desmond," Sanders explained.

"JFM, Agent Desmond," I offered.

Desmond looked from Sanders back to me. "JFM? What in the hell's *JFM*?"

"Just fuckin' magic," I said.

Desmond and Brinks both looked at me with incredulous expressions as Sanders glared at me.

* * *

In no time at all, Agent Sanders and I were on a flight headed back to Nevis Corners. Before we left Chicago, we'd somehow survived a heated conference that included Sanders' supervisor via phone, though I hardly blamed either Kip Desmond or Chuck Denton for being angry. As field office management, they had the dubious task of explaining to their superiors why recent affairs has gone so badly, although Desmond also had to account for the deaths of three good men.

I was experienced at being under fire, but I never got accustomed to the casualties. One minute they're alive, maybe standing shoulder-to-shoulder right next to you, and the next minute they're not. The surreal nature of it remained forever stark in my mind.

One serious problem was that nobody seemed to have any adequate explanations for what had happened. And worse yet, we were still no closer to divining the location, or fate, of Maria Edwards.

To hell with fate; I was determined to find her.

Failure wasn't an option; there were two kids who desperately needed to have their mother back.

I clenched my fists until my knuckles cracked, and Agent Sanders regarded me warily from her aisle seat next to me.

"Getting upset's not going to help our situation," she admonished.

I waited until a flight attendant passed by, before replying. "Neither is wasting time sitting on a flight headed back to Nevis Corners."

"Rough day at the office?" asked the fellow to my right who'd been lucky enough to command the window seat.

His slicked-back hair and Cheshire cat grin reminded me of car salesmen and lawyers, neither of which I was particularly fond. I regarded him with a hard stare and he quickly returned to his iPad.

Sanders gently nudged my left arm, and I turned to glare at her. She motioned to the steno pad that she'd been scribbling on.

"Focus, please," she whispered.

I looked down at her notepad where she'd written *The Facts and Leads* at the top. Beneath that were the two names that Thomas Gibbons had rattled off in his head before his demise in the patrol car, as well as the other names we'd been provided by Clive Bernard. There were also a host of key players under a government and corporate heading, including state and local officials, and of course, key figures within Nuclegene Corporation, including Bernard.

It was all very interesting. However, one final notation caught my eye in particular; one Sanders had circled twice.

It succinctly stated: *Hit man shows up at crime scene and investigation site. Inside leaks?*

Leaks. That bothered me. Not so much that there might be a leak, but that there might be more than one.

I looked up at Sanders and frowned.

She nodded sagely.

I hoped she was mistaken, but recent events pointed in that direction.

CHAPTER 11

It was late in the evening by the time we arrived back at the Nevis Corners FBI office. Almost immediately, we ran another sweep of the list of names through the bureau and Homeland Security databases. In the end, we were no closer to divining the figures behind the partial names, Hadrian or Wenzel.

"What if it's not two, but one?" I asked as a group of us, including Chuck Denton, perched around Sanders' desk area for a brainstorming session. "You know, like Hadrian Wenzel."

"Or Wenzel Hadrian," added Agent Collins, her eyes meeting mine.

I stared back at her, momentarily appreciating her engaging blue eyes. "A fair point," I said.

"Worth checking," Sanders admitted, though when I glanced back at her she was staring at me with a hint of disapproval.

"What?" I asked.

Everyone exchanged looks at me and then back at Sanders.

Denton cleared his throat. "Listen up, I know it's damned late, but there's no time to waste. Let's get on it. Collins, on a hunch, try cross-checking our list of names against Immigration's database. Foster, check Interpol."

Everyone quickly dispersed, leaving Sanders and me sitting at her desk. She typed away at her workstation keyboard with a terse set to her jaw.

"Anything I can do to help?" I asked.

"No," she replied somewhat coolly.

I was no dummy. I could tell something was bothering her.

"You seem a little put out with me right now," I said.

She stopped typing and turned to stare into my eyes. Despite appearing angry, she still had beautiful hazel eyes; perhaps more so than Collins' blue ones.

"Put out? You think I'm put out, do you? Well, call me short-sighted, but maybe you could try *Googling* something useful instead of trading *googly-eyes* with Agent Collins."

"A little tension between you two?" I asked.

"Between *her* and *me*?" she seethed in a whispered tone.

She growled and returned to typing—no, rather hammering—on her keyboard.

I started to say something, but thought better of it. Instead, I moved to a nearby unoccupied workstation with a copy of the notes that Sanders had made.

"Could you sign me on here?" I asked.

Sanders gave me a cold look, though she signed into the system for me before silently returning to her own keyboard.

Saying nothing, I opened up Google, resigned that I'd probably never understand the depths of the feminine mystique.

After a few minutes, Sanders looked up with a start.

"I've got a hit."

I rolled my chair across the floor toward her as Agents Foster and Collins rushed over to her desk.

"Whatcha' got?" Foster asked.

"I have municipal parking tickets for a Hadrian Wenzel in Henderson, Nevada," Sanders blurted. "They've got his driver's license info, which gives us an address. I'm cross-referencing with other databases now."

Agent Denton peeked out from his office.

"Foster, get some plane tickets to Las Vegas for you, Sanders, and Bringer. I want you on the next plane out, and I don't care if we have to bump a congressman to do it," he ordered. "I'll get on the phone with our local bureau office and make arrangements for tactical support."

Sanders nodded as she clicked her mouse like a madwoman on the screen options before her.

"And Sanders," Denton cautioned. "This time, you'd better secure whoever you nab out there. I want live people to interrogate this time."

Sanders looked up with a frown. "Yes, sir."

I snatched the plastic bottle of sports drink from the corner of her desk and upended it. I had to make sure that my brain was charged up this time.

Then I recalled the syringes of vitamin supplements that I'd taken from Maria's refrigerator. Yet another reason that I needed her back safely; I had no idea what the proper mixture was.

I made my way to the small break room on the other side of the office. I'd stored one of the syringes containing my vitamin mixture inside a small thermos in the small employee refrigerator.

I looked around to ensure I was alone.

While rolling up my shirtsleeve, I belatedly realized that it was still stained with dirt and grime from the Chicago streets.

I wasn't about to contribute to another debacle like that, if I could help it. But then, what could I have done better to prevent what had happened?

I popped the cap off the syringe and tried to decide the best self-injection method. All that I'd ever learned about injections was back in the army when they had demonstrated how to jam an atropine needle into my thigh in case of chemical agent exposure.

"Are you a diabetic?" Sanders asked.

I winced and gazed in her direction. I hadn't even heard

her enter the room. What was she, a trained ninja?

"It's a vitamin solution," I replied.

She frowned as she approached me.

"Please tell me that's not an illegal substance," she prodded with a disapproving tone.

I gave her a wan look. "Maria Edwards gave it to me. She said it would help with my abilities."

By the surprised look on her face, she hadn't expected that response.

"Give me that," she said as she reached out for the syringe. "You'll probably end up putting an air bubble into your bloodstream. That's all we need is for you to have a massive coronary or a stroke."

I adopted a dubious expression. "So, you're a nurse, too?"

"For your information, I used to volunteer at my father's neighborhood clinic as a teenager. I know my way around a needle and more."

Sanders was just full of surprises.

"Well then, thanks, doc," I chimed.

She injected the solution in a practiced manner, though not quite as seamlessly as Maria had done.

"For the time being, you'd better let me give these to you," she suggested. "At least until someone can show you how to do it properly."

I handed her the needle cover and she dropped the empty syringe back into my thermos.

"Rule number one—don't reuse your needles," she instructed.

"There's a few that Maria had already prepared back at my hotel room," I said.

"How frequently?"

"Daily for now, if I recall correctly what Maria said," I replied.

"Our flight is in two hours. We're each going to pack an overnight bag, just in case," she said. "Bring one syringe with you, but put it in your jacket. We won't have to deal with customs; I can get us past that easily enough."

"Thanks a lot, Sanders," I said.

"Well, you did sort of save my life again today," she said. "So, I guess I owe you one."

She spared me a momentary look of complete sincerity before her visage returned to that of the consummate professional. She pressed the thermos into my hands.

"Come on," she said. "We don't have time to waste. We'll try to catch a nap on our flight."

On the way to the airport, Sanders went by her apartment and then stopped by my hotel so I could hastily pick up a change of clothes. We met Agent Ben Foster at the terminal and fortunately didn't have to wait long before we boarded our flight.

Once again, I was vexed over the sense of futility from waiting, as if precious time was progressively sifting through our fingers. Still, I was determined that this journey was going to be more successful than our last.

Then I recalled that the road to hell was paved with good intentions.

* * *

I fell asleep sometime during the flight and dreamt that I was sitting on an airplane next to both Sanders and Foster. However, all of the other passengers had faces that were devoid of features. There were literally just pale white voids where their faces formerly resided.

I looked to my left where Sanders was quietly talking to herself about a host of tasks and ideas. I looked to my right where Foster calmly recited a list of items that all sounded like articles one would pack for a trip. Then a din of voices slowly built around me and I found myself unable to pick out a single, lucid voice. The din grew to a cacophony until it was like dozens of men's and women's voices practically screaming in my head.

"Shut up!" I yelled, clapping my hands over my ears.

Then I jerked awake.

Sanders stared at me with concern.

"Bad dream?" she asked. "Your face is sweating."

I looked to my right, but Foster was leaned back into his seat with his eyes closed, seemingly at ease.

"Nah, I'm fine," I said evasively and excused myself to go to the bathroom to splash cold water on my face.

The remainder of the flight was thankfully uneventful, but it was as if I could still subtly *sense* a host of voices in the back of my mind. Slowly, and quite thankfully, the sensation abated.

By the time we landed at McCarran International Airport in Las Vegas it was close to midnight. The field office supervisor from the Las Vegas bureau, Sid Prescott, and an agent named Letitia Hansen met us at the terminal. During the introductions, both agents considered me suspiciously. Either they hadn't expected a "civilian" to be part of our little group, or they'd already heard about the debacle in Chicago.

On the drive to the local bureau office, the agents informed us that they'd already formed a small task force in conjunction with both Las Vegas and Henderson municipal police departments.

We left our luggage at the FBI offices and immediately suited up in bulletproof vests. More than once, Prescott asked Sanders if I was actually supposed to be in harm's way, given my status of being "under the bureau's protection."

"He's far more useful to us in the field, I assure you," Sanders said.

The drive down the Great Basin Highway was quicker than I thought it would be. By the time we passed south of the Nevada State College campus, the area looked rather desolated, though more likely due to the imposing darkness.

"Are we still in Henderson?" I asked.

"Yes, although we're actually just as close to Boulder City as Henderson," Agent Hansen remarked.

"What else can you tell us about the residence?" Sanders asked.

"It's a small farm. One of our best field agents, Mike Carter, is already staging the tactical team around the site," Prescott informed us.

"Farming? Around here?" I asked.

Iowa was one thing, but arid Nevada seemed outrageous for farming.

"Sounds odd, I know. Nevada's the driest state in the nation," Prescott said. "In fact, much of the surrounding area is little more than uninhabited, sagebrush-covered desert. Historically, we're better known for silver mining operations."

"My grandparents grew melons in Boulder City when I was growing up," Hansen said. "It takes some additional watering, but you can do it successfully."

Farming in the desert.

And to think that reading minds and blocking bullets in mid-air was supposed to sound strange.

"Listen, before we arrive on site, there's a couple of things I'd like to know," Prescott said. "I've seen the news coverage on TV of what happened earlier today in Chicago. Your supervisor, Agent Denton, was a little evasive when I spoke with him, so I took the liberty of placing a call to my peer in Chicago, Agent Desmond. He said what should've been a routine search and arrest turned into a balls-to-the-wall gun fight."

"It was both unexpected and unfortunate," Sanders said diplomatically.

"This whole situation seems a little strange at this point and I just want to know what we might be walking into, Agent Sanders," Prescott continued. "And while you're at it, why don't you explain to me why Denton was so insistent about my bringing a cooler filled with sports drink with us. We're not a catering service, you know."

He had a point. Frankly, I couldn't blame the guy.

I looked at Sanders and then stared out the car window to the darkness beyond.

"Honestly, Agent Prescott, it's more complicated than

you might think," Sanders said.

CHAPTER 12

We pulled off the highway some distance from our destination and proceeded down a dirt road in the middle of nowhere. A few police cars, a Ford sedan, and an oversized RV that was stenciled with *Las Vegas Mobile Tactical Command Center* were situated along the side of the road.

Inside the command center, numerous law enforcement officials prepared their gear while others watched over video surveillance screens arrayed along one wall of the vehicle.

We were introduced to the tactical commander, a Las Vegas police major named Duggar, as well as Special Agent Mike Carter. Both were attired in body armor. A quick scan of everyone quickly suggested that body armor was the uniform of the day.

It appeared that nobody was taking any chances with the operation.

"We've already created a perimeter of men a couple of hundred yards outside the boundaries of the property," Duggar explained. "Everyone will wear a wire, so when the order is given, we'll close in together from all sides. Snipers are arrayed in three locations that give us a sound periphery of fire coverage. The only structures appear to be the two-story house, two small outbuildings, and a large barn. There are two propane tanks to be cautious of; one on the front side of the house, and another along one side of the large barn. The back side of the property is a series of vegetable patches and watering apparatus."

All in all, it seemed as though everything was in order and everyone seemed prepared. That should've reassured me, but after Chicago, I just kept wondering what we might have missed; though SWAT tactics were hardly my specialty.

You never know everything you need to.

It'd felt that way when I was deployed overseas back in my army days, as well. It was good to plan and prepare, but few arrangements survived the chaos and dynamic events that took place in a live combat zone.

I learned that no battle plan was sound beyond first contact with the enemy.

But those days were over, weren't they?

I noticed Foster and Sanders being wired with those Secret Service-looking earpieces and microphones. I rubbed at my ear where my earpiece was tickling me.

It was nearly eleven o'clock by the time that Sanders, Foster, and I finished gearing up. Most of the tactical team had already deployed around the farm's perimeter. Only a small entry team accompanied us.

A tactical van transported us back to the main highway and then along the couple of hundred yards of gravel road where the farm was located. In order to maximize stealth, we walked the short distance from where the van was parked to the farm property.

It was a quiet, dark night with no moon, and there was little if any traffic on the gravel road behind us. We moved off of the gravel to the sandy side of the road to minimize the noise from our footfalls.

We made our way down the narrow dirt driveway leading up to the main house.

It was a large, rustic-looking two-story farm home with 1950s era architecture. There appeared to be no lights on in the house and a lone white Ford Explorer was parked at the side of the house close by the large barn. The entire place had a slightly abandoned feeling to it, though part of that might've been the nocturnal hour.

Agents Foster and Carter made their way to the back of the house with their tactical team, while Sanders, Prescott, and I quietly approached the front of the house with our four-man tactical team. As we reached the propane tank that was maybe a hundred feet from the house, I lifted my hand for everyone to halt.

"What?" Sanders whispered to me in an urgent tone.

"I've got an idea," I said. "Wait here until I signal for you."

Sanders started to protest, but I pointed meaningfully at my head and ear with one hand. She nodded and motioned for everyone to squat behind the propane tank.

It was then that the utter absurdity of using a potentially explosive tank for cover occurred to me, but I let it slide.

"What the hell's he doing?" Prescott quietly demanded.

I ignored him and made my way to the old, wooden front steps that led up to the wide porch.

"Prescott here," he said over the comm link. "We're halted out front, just beyond the front porch. Stand by."

I stopped, crouched down near the front steps, and opened my thoughts. Unlike my experience at the Nuclegene Corporate offices, my ability only took a couple of seconds to respond.

A tingling sensation flowed through my head, and picked up on multiple thoughts at once. Picking through the voices, I realized that it was Sanders and the rest of the team behind me. I adjusted my concentration and envisioned a sweeping pattern ahead of me.

I immediately picked up two streams of thought.

...why I can't fall sleep very easily nowadays, came one thought.

...wish I could just see my children one more time, came another.

My heart skipped a beat and my concentration nearly broke completely.

One of the people had to be Maria!

I quickly made my way back to the propane tank.

"Well?" Sanders insisted.

"Two people; both awake," I said. "One has to be Maria."

"What the---" one of the tactical team members began.

"Go," Prescott ordered over the comm. "Repeat, we're green."

"Let's do this," one of the team members added.

The four-man entry team and Prescott immediately charged up to the front porch. Sanders and I rose to follow by the time a small battering ram slammed against the front door with a loud cracking sound as the door banged inward.

A split second later, a loud boom went off in the midst of a bright flash.

My arms flew up while envisioning an imaginary wall before me as a cloud of flame and shards of wood shot toward us.

I felt the impact of intense heat, but the wall of flames wrapped around Sanders and me and kept going.

"Shit!" Sanders screamed.

Then my mind felt like a giant hammer abruptly struck it, and I staggered but managed to remain standing. Something at my feet caught my attention and I looked down at the metal battering ram while simultaneously feeling Sanders' body pressed against my back.

Crap! The metal ram must have blown back at us.

The scene around us was utter chaos. The comm was screaming with voices.

Maria! I had to get to Maria.

"Stay here!" I yelled and charged toward the ragged, gaping hole that used to be the front door and front façade of the porch.

I silently pleaded, *please don't be dead. Please don't be dead!*

"Logan!" Sanders shouted from behind.

I hit the front porch at a dead run. Fortunately, I was able to negotiate a smoldering hole in the wooden porch by the light of flames around me. The interior of the house was a mess and spot fires had started along two walls in the living room.

I whipped out a flashlight that I'd procured from the command post and tried to open my mind again to any stray thoughts. It was difficult to concentrate between the barrage of voices in my earpiece, the roar of fire that continued to build inside the house, and the building scream of sirens outside.

…can't get loose, came a stray frantic thought.

…house is going up, came another.

Great, I was hustling through yet another rapidly burning home.

God, I hated house fires.

I dodged past a small end table obstructing my path in the hallway.

…get to him before the tunnel, came a vague thought.

Tunnel?

"Maria!" I yelled.

I was halfway down a narrow smoke-filled hallway when the dim silhouette of a tall, burly fellow rounded the corner. I quickly focused upon what appeared to be a shotgun that was leveled at me.

Shield, I thought as I dropped my flashlight and lifted both of my palms up before me.

Two flashes came in quick succession, lighting the hallway, even as loud gunshots nearly deafened me.

My head felt like it was practically splitting open, but I still sensed, almost felt, the mass of pellets before me. They felt almost tactile somehow.

A flood of anger surged inside of me and I yelled while thrusting my palms away from me. The man made a gurgling noise as his body flew backward against a wall at the end of the hallway with a resounding thud. The telltale sound of pellets ricocheting against both the wall and through glass immediately followed.

I grabbed my flashlight and illuminated the smoky

hallway to reveal the man's bloody and bullet-riddled body slumped on the floor.

"Help!" came a scream from my left.

The wooden door to my left failed to yield when I tried twisting the door handle. I backed against the wall and swift-kicked at it instead.

The door flew open and banged against the interior wall, revealing Maria on a bed before me. She was fully clothed, but appeared to be frantically tugging against a chain that was attached to the floor.

"Maria!" I shouted, rushing into the dimly lit room.

Thank God, she was alive!

I heard a roar behind me and felt intense heat. I managed to slam the door shut just as flames shot into view before me.

I turned back to her, and her eyes were wild with fear as she practically leapt into my arms. It was hard to miss the bruises on her face and the nearly blackened eye indicating that someone had abused her; a fact that sent a pang of rage through me.

"Oh, Logan," she half-wept. "Thank God you found me!"

"I know," I said, silently thankful that holding out hope hadn't been in vain. "We've gotta' get you the hell outta' here."

I pulled away from her to see that a set of metal leg cuffs were fastened around her ankles and locked to a chain that had been secured into the floor.

"The man that took me has the keys," she stammered.

Oh, crap. The man that I just killed and left in the hallway that's currently ablaze.

I activated my comm link as the small nearby table lamp started flickering.

"This is Bringer. I'm in a room on the first floor and I found Maria," I half-shouted as I assessed the room.

No windows.

"I don't have an exit; the hallway's engulfed," I added, noting that smoke was pouring in from underneath the door.

I glanced up and saw that the paint was bubbling on the ceiling as it smoldered.

Oh, shit.

"Bringer! Fire trucks are on scene now," came Sanders' voice.

I knew that I didn't have time to wait for the fire crews. Besides, I also needed to get Maria loose somehow, too.

Then I spied a heavy oak dresser across the room and got an idea.

"Get people ready on the back side of the house," I ordered. "I need somebody with bolt cutters in order to free Maria. Come in as soon as you see my exit."

"What exit?" Sanders demanded.

I grabbed Maria in my arms and positioned her behind me. Fortunately, her chain permitted just enough slack for that.

She tightly wrapped her arms around my midsection and started crying.

Part of the ceiling above the door gave away and flames licked into the room as I concentrated on the oak dresser. I held out my hands and focused on mentally grabbing it, just as I'd done with the garbage bin outside that Chicago apartment.

It rattled and began shaking as I reached out to it with my thoughts. Something in my mind seemed to click into place because I almost *felt* the solidness of the dresser under my hands.

The room filled with smoke and increasing heat, and I felt my body pouring with sweat. There was no way that I was going to let Maria die in this house. The very thought of it made me so angry that I wanted to crush something.

I jerked my hands toward me as if trying to cast the dresser across the room to my right.

The oak dresser seemed to leap up into the air from its resting place and launched across the room in a blur to smash against the wall. A resounding crash accompanied boards snapping in half and sheet rock being rent asunder by the wooden projective.

I noted via the nearly four-foot-across hole in the wall that the dresser had rolled across the back yard some distance from the house.

"Holy shit!" yelled somebody outside.

"Get in here!" I yelled at the top of my lungs.

My attention diverted to the ceiling where flames burst above our heads. The lamp in the room flickered one final time and then went out, leaving only the flames in the ceiling to light the room in a hellish-looking hue.

As two tactical team members squeezed through the hole, I held my hands up and concentrated on another shield.

"What are you---" one officer began.

"Just get her outta' here!" I yelled before trying to refocus my thoughts.

I yanked the earpiece out of my ear to avoid the chatter coming in over the comm.

Shield, shield, shield, I thought over and over as I held my palms up before me.

I imagined that I was smoothing out a giant piece of elastic glass before me, and I immediately saw the flames lapping against the invisible barrier. I sensed intense heat in my head, almost feverish-feeling, as well as a prickling and numbing sensation in my hands.

"Don't worry, ma'am," an officer cooed reassuringly. "We're getting you out of here."

"Mother, Mary, and Joseph," I heard a man gasp behind me.

I spared a quick look behind me to see a tactical team member shining his light at me and staring at me wide-eyed like I was the devil or something.

"Hurry up!" I barked, to which the man snapped out of his trance to help his partner.

I heard a clanking sound, which I hoped was Maria's chain tether being severed with bolt cutters.

"Go! Get her outta' here!" one of the tactical team members shouted.

My barrier was quickly being flanked by a host of flames as sweat poured down my face, though whether from the searing heat or my growing sense of exhaustion, I had no idea. The only certainty in my mind was I was losing the battle before me, and I didn't think I could hold the shield for more than another minute before I collapsed.

"Clear!" shouted a voice behind me.

"Logan!" Sanders shouted somewhere outside. "Get the hell out of there!"

It felt like my body was cooking both outside and inside my head as I collapsed the shield before me. The ceiling completely caved in on that side of the room as black smoke generated an eerie cloud around me. I looked down at my hands in astonishment to see that flames remained suspended above my palms, floating above them like macabre, haunting spirits.

I felt momentarily transfixed by them.

I flapped my hands to extinguish the flames, coughing spasmodically and nearly falling to the floor in weakness. I lurched forward, placing my body closer to the hole in the wall, only to feel multiple sets of hands grabbing at me.

My body went momentarily airborne before being dragged across the rough ground outside.

When I came to a stop, an oxygen mask was pressed to my face amidst a half dozen flashlights shining down upon me.

Sanders face appeared before me.

"Welcome back, hero," she teased.

The sounds of radio chatter, sirens, and multiple shouting voices created a roar of noise around me. Yet, one man standing nearby managed to shout above the rancor.

"That's the most amazing damned thing I've ever seen! Just who the hell is he, anyway?"

"Him? He's Captain JFM," Sanders half-shouted.

"What's JFM?" asked another man.

"Just Fucking Magic," she answered with a smirk as her hazel eyes peered into mine.

I chuckled despite myself.

"Speaking of magic," I began. "Look around for some kind of tunnel under the house. I'll bet you'll find a disappearing trick."

CHAPTER 13

The night's events had nearly resulted in another debacle. At least my competency with my talents had improved somewhat. My thought-reading had divined a relatively simple tunnel system underneath the house with tunnels leading to a couple of useful escape points hundreds of yards from the property's structures.

Best of all, I'd found Maria alive.

God, I'm exhausted.

Even after consuming two containers of sports drinks and taking a long, hot shower at our hotel, my body still felt like it'd been run over by a truck. Of course, it was well after two in the morning, and I'd just used more of my talent in one day than I had since first discovering my abilities.

And yet, now that Maria was resting safe and sound under protective custody just down the hall, I also felt relieved, nearly giddy, as I wrapped a towel around my bare waist.

I plopped down on the edge of my bed and momentarily considered placing a call to Lexi to see how she and the rest of the family were doing. That's when the time of night returned to the forefront of my mind, so I placed my phone back onto the nightstand instead.

"How the hell did I get into all of this in the first place?"

I asked aloud.

Honestly, the past week or so had felt like a blur in my mind.

Maybe I was simply exhausted from the events of recent days. It felt like I was back in a combat zone all over again.

A knock at my room's door roused me from my reverie and I slipped on a pair of sweatpants and T-shirt.

Agent Sanders stood before me wearing a pair of jeans and FBI-labeled sweatshirt. Ever the consummate professional agent, her badge and service pistol were strapped to her waistband.

I couldn't help but grin.

"May I come in, Bringer?" she asked.

"Sure," I replied, stepping aside for her to enter.

She paused, as if considering the bed, but then moved to a chair situated before a small courtesy desk across the room.

"Want some Gatorade?" I asked, taking note of the bucket of ice and half dozen plastic containers of sports drinks on the dresser.

"No, thanks," she replied. "I see they took my request seriously," she said with an arched brow.

I casually grabbed one of the containers and poured the contents over a glass of ice.

"I thought you might finally be trying to get some sleep," I said.

"I would've liked that," she agreed somewhat forlornly. "However, I just got off the phone with Agent Denton back at our office. We've got a small problem."

That didn't sound good.

"What kind of problem?" I asked, perching on the edge of the bed.

"It seems that our exploits on the streets of Chicago were captured by a pedestrian with a cell phone camera," she began. "Which, in turn, made its way onto both the Internet and blogs. Naturally, the news media picked it up, and it's playing on major news networks."

I was generally a pro-media kind of guy, but these were

particularly sensitive circumstances.

"Fortunately, there's a lot of conjecture as to whether the video was real or merely doctored up with some video editing software to perpetrate a hoax," she said.

"Okay. That sounds more encouraging," I said cautiously.

"So far, the bureau is maintaining a 'no comment' approach for the time being; although Denton said he had to discreetly report the facts to some bureau brass higher up the chain. In turn, a report made its way to both the CIA and the NSA," Sanders continued. "And suffice to say, there's some people who really want to meet you when we get back to Nevis Corners."

"Shit," I muttered.

"Yeah, real shit," she solemnly agreed.

And to think that, just a few minutes ago, I'd felt like things had been ballooning out of control. Now, it seemed that we'd just transferred from a balloon to a rocket.

"What do we do?" I asked.

Sanders sighed. "I don't see that we have a lot of options right now. But I can't help feeling that containment of information about you is about to become a lot harder."

"And with people who aren't necessarily as concerned about my wellbeing," I added acidly.

I'd run across some CIA operatives back in the Middle East and they weren't necessarily the straightforward types. In fact, they operated in a lot of gray areas that most Americans had no clue about.

One thing for sure, I knew I didn't want to get mixed up with them.

"We'll catch a flight back first thing this morning. And don't worry, Bringer, we're not going to hang you out to dry," she tried to reassure me.

I stared into her eyes and noted a determined look of sincerity. Sanders was definitely the *real deal*; somebody guided by her conviction and a genuine desire to help and protect people.

However, she didn't know certain clandestine divisions within our government like I did, and she had no idea of the kind of nefarious influence they wielded. They might be closer to what we'd been facing with the mysterious Continuance Corporation thus far; except these guys wrapped themselves in an American flag when they found it convenient to further their cause.

"Bringer?" Sanders asked.

"Yeah, I heard you," I said. "Thanks, Sanders. I appreciate all you've done."

She rose from her chair, walked over to me, and placed the cool palm of her hand against the side of my face as I looked into her eyes.

"You're pretty amazing, Captain JFM. And I owe you more than I could ever repay," she softly affirmed.

I reached up to cover her hand with my own and replied, "My pleasure."

Then she gently withdrew her hand.

"Try to get some sleep," she urged as she opened the door to leave. "I'll give you a wake-up call around six-ish."

Yeah, as if I was going to be able to sleep now.

* * *

I must've fallen asleep while lying on the bed contemplating my situation because the alarm on my cell phone startled me awake. I shaved and got dressed just before Agent Sanders knocked on my door.

She briefed me on the loose ends we'd be leaving behind. Then I asked her to give me my vitamin injection before we checked out.

Once again, I thought of Maria.

As I left the room with overnight bag in hand, I stopped and looked down the hallway to where two police officers were stationed outside Maria's room.

"Just a minute," I told Sanders, dropping my bag onto the floor.

I lightly knocked on Maria's door and waited. Granted, it was still pretty early, but I just had to see her before I left.

"Just a minute," I heard her voice.

She must've paused to look through the peephole because I heard the series of locks hurriedly clicking before the door flung open.

Her smile was priceless, and she hugged me tightly to her.

"Oh, Logan, thank you, thank you," she half-cried.

I wrapped my arms around her and swiveled my head to softly kiss her on her bruised cheek.

"I'm so glad that I found you," I said, leaving the addition of "in time" unsaid.

The truth was, finding her alive made everything that I'd endured seem so worth it. Though after seeing how she had been treated, I would've liked the opportunity to work that guy over more before I killed him.

"Are we leaving already?" she asked.

"No, Agent Sanders and I have to head back early," I said. "But you're leaving later this morning, I'm told. You'll be back home to your children by lunchtime or so. And this time, you'll be safe. Sanders assured me the police will be stationed outside your home 24/7."

"I don't think I'll ever truly feel safe again," she said.

"Now, now. None of that," I said. "Maria, before I go, I need to know what your captors wanted from you."

She sighed and pulled from our embrace slightly, looking remarkably composed for a person who'd just endured what she had. Though, in reality, her life had probably been traumatic ever since the Wallace Building explosion.

"They kept asking me about our company's genetic research and the treatments you'd been taking," she said. "One time, they even asked what personal information I knew about you. Fortunately, I didn't have a lot to tell them. I mean, outside of your patient file, that is. And they wanted to know how much progress the treatments had progressed prior to our office's destruction. In fact, just a few hours before you rescued me, that man wanted to know how far your abilities had progressed."

My jaw tightened.

"How many people did you see?"

"Just that man," she replied. "Though I never once heard him say his name. The only name I overheard him say was one time when he was on the phone outside the room I was locked in. It was a woman…he called her Miss Folker, or maybe Volker, I think."

"Thanks, Maria. That's really helpful," I said.

At least it was something more than we had before. I suppose I should've tried not to kill that guy with the shotgun, in retrospect. But then, I've never been particularly cautious when being down range from someone who's trying to kill me.

"Bringer, we have to get going," Sanders prompted.

I'd been oblivious to the fact she was standing next to me. I must've been more exhausted than I'd thought.

"I'll see you soon, Maria," I said.

She nodded.

"Logan, I can tell you're getting stronger," Maria offered.

"Hey, I'm taking my vitamins," I quipped, and turned to follow Sanders down the hall.

* * *

I managed to call Lexi at the airport terminal while waiting to board our flight home. Fortunately, she, the kids, and my parents were all well. She told me that a police car was stationed outside of our parents' house where they were staying, and one was always close by when they left the house. At least the FBI had been as good as their word on that.

Lexi had a host of questions for me, but I remained relatively vague; the fact we were talking over an unsecured line being foremost in my mind.

Geez, it was like being back in the military all over again.

Naturally, before I was able to finish my conversation with Lexi, my mother wanted to chat. I'd expected the usual motherly concern that all sons receive from the women who brought them into the world, but this time Mom surprised me with a topic that came out of left field.

"Your father and I aren't the only ones worried about you, Logan," Mom said. "One of your old army friends, that nice congressman from New York, Paul Criswell, called to ask how you were."

Paul Criswell? I hadn't heard that name in months. For some unknown reason, rather than calling me, he used to call Mom once in a while during my cancer treatment just to check up on me. Every time I'd tried calling him back, he'd always been away from his Capitol Hill office, or I'd gone directly to voicemail.

Paul had been a member of my fire team back in Afghanistan. He'd made sergeant faster than anyone I'd ever seen. Of course, he deserved it. He was one of the best soldiers over there; all business in the field but somebody who had your back whether you liked him or not.

Paul was definitely "good people" and we'd seen eye-to-eye from day one. We'd been tight overseas but had lost touch with each other after we redeployed back home.

No harm there. Frankly, that sort of thing happened a lot more than people thought. It's just the way that life wrapped you up and swept you onward sometimes.

Of course, life had worked out far better for Paul than most of the guys in my fire team; he was one of only two in my squad who hadn't either contracted, or died from, cancer since their return to the States. Better yet, he'd been the most successful of all of us, having used his wartime experience to ride a wave of patriotism all the way into office during his first congressional campaign.

Lucky bastard.

"Logan? Are you there?" Mom asked with concern.

"Yeah, sorry, Mom," I replied. "I was just thinkin' I hadn't heard from Paul in quite awhile, that's all. What did he have to say?"

"It was so nice of him to call," Mom recounted fondly. "He said he'd been monitoring the recent news reports about the terrible building explosion, and that he was so happy you hadn't been in the building. He said that he wanted to find out if you were feeling okay."

That's strange. Once again, why the hell didn't he just call me?

"Did you give him my phone number and ask him to give me a call?" I asked.

"Of course. It was the first thing I offered, though I know I've given it to him before," Mom replied. "He thanked me, but said he didn't want to be a bother with all that you were probably going through right now."

Then Sanders waved over to me that our flight was boarding, so I had to cut my call with Mom short.

CHAPTER 14

The flight back to Nevis Corners felt like the shortest in my life, and I was well aware why.

More interest from the feds.

Although it wasn't until Sanders and I stepped into the FBI office downtown that my nerves turned completely on edge. We were hastily summoned into a large, nearby conference room filled with people wearing impeccable suits.

Everyone rose as soon as Sanders and I walked into the room, and Agent Denton moved to greet us first by shaking hands with both Sanders and me.

"Welcome back, you two," he said. "Good work down in Las Vegas."

I turned my attention to the five other strangers in the room and gave them a hard look. To my surprise, they regarded me like I was some kind of new scientific discovery, which unnerved me slightly.

A tall, slim dark-haired woman in a tailored women's suit stepped forward to shake my hand.

"Mr. Bringer, I'm Yasmine Prichard, Special Agent in Charge of Domestic Affairs at the Central Intelligence Agency," the woman offered in a practiced manner.

I was surprised that the CIA had developed a domestic affairs division. To my knowledge, they typically dealt with foreign intelligence issues.

A man who appeared to be in his mid-forties and wearing a dark wool suit with red bow tie stepped forward to greet me next.

"Hello, Mr. Bringer," the man said. "I'm Bob Tevin, Deputy Director of the National Security Agency and Central Security Service."

Next, a tall man who appeared to be in his late fifties stepped forward to shake my hand. His hawkish-looking features and furrowed eyebrows looked somewhat amusing to me.

"Mr. Bringer, I'm Mark Wainright, Deputy Director from FBI headquarters in Washington, DC," the man said. "I've read a lot about you. Ex-army, eh? Thanks for your service."

I nodded respectfully, but repressed a sigh. I realized people were being polite and displaying their national pride when they thanked me for my military service.

I was proud to have volunteered for the army.

However, few people knew what I'd done just to survive, or how many people I'd killed in the line of duty. Even worse were the occasional collateral damage mistakes on fire control missions in the heat of battle.

Then there was the subsequent guilt for having survived when so many others, some who seemed much more deserving than me, didn't.

It's hard to overcome powerful thoughts and feelings like those when you return stateside. You can hardly metabolize the scope of it all, much less turn it off like a light switch. It was one of the few things they never trained us to confront or deal with in the army.

I dunno. It just seemed strange to be thanked by someone for all that.

Of course, I was a realist, too. I was much happier being a survivor than one of the deceased. Hell, the people downrange from me had been trying to kill me just as much as I'd been trying to kill them.

Again, too bad some of the troops I'd served with overseas hadn't been so fortunate.

Too many absent friends.

For that reason alone, I'd grown sick of memorial services by the time I'd returned stateside.

I waited as Agent Sanders shook hands with everyone. I discreetly opened my mind and tried to listen in on the minds around me as everyone took seats around the conference table.

…looks perfectly ordinary to me, one thought surfaced.

…can't believe the report from Chicago, came another.

…if the video footage was real or not?

…wonder if he can read minds?

I focused on the source of that last thought and turned to look directly into Special Agent Prichard's brown eyes.

Say something about the weather if you can hear me.

Prichard regarded me intently as I casually continued to scan the other faces around the table. No need to show my hand at this stage in the game, I figured.

Yeah, some game this was turning out to be.

"There's coffee across the room, if anyone wants it," Denton said.

"Let's get down to it, Denton," Wainright insisted. "Mr. Bringer, I'd be remiss if I didn't begin by saying that you've moved from a person of interest to a person of appreciation to the FBI. And on behalf of the Bureau, I'd like to thank you for the generous assistance that you've graciously volunteered to us in pursuit of terrorists related to the Wallace Building bombing."

Click-click.

My eyes immediately went to the ballpoint ink pen that Prichard was twirling around her fingers.

"Alleged terrorists," Prichard corrected.

That seemed to raise Wainright's ire.

"I don't know what you folks in the CIA think, Special Agent Prichard, but blowing up a building full of civilians is viewed as a terrorist act by the FBI," he said.

"Or perhaps corporate espionage," Prichard shot back.

"Fine. But Bestand Gesellschaft, or should I say Continuance Corporation, is a foreign corporation that, I might point out, no longer operates in the open," Wainright noted.

"Perhaps we shouldn't become mired in the semantics of the investigation right now," Tevin said. "I think we would be best served by focusing on Mr. Bringer and the contribution that he has provided to the FBI thus far."

Click-click.

"Indeed," Prichard said. "Though I would hardly offer Mr. Bringer my accolades after seeing the destruction and reading the casualty report from the FBI's botched Chicago operation," she countered.

"Interesting point. And how's that latest *regime-change business* going over in Afghanistan for the CIA right now, Ms. Prichard?" I asked matter-of-factly.

"*Bringer,*" Sanders whispered harshly.

However, Deputy Director Wainright adopted a satisfied expression.

"Touché, I believe," he muttered while nodding deferentially to me. "Three successive regime changes in less than twelve years begin to look a little tiresome."

Okay, so maybe Wainright seemed mildly odd, and he dressed somewhat dated-looking, but I was growing to like him.

Click-click, click-click.

I also found Ms. Prichard's pen-clicking quickly getting on my nerves.

"Very well, then," Prichard conceded. "Let's discuss Mr. Bringer, shall we?"

Agent Denton provided a brief recount of the Wallace Building explosion, as well as the initial stages of the FBI's investigation.

"However, it's highly irregular that Mr. Bringer would be sheltered by the FBI, and in fact, almost be treated as a consultant of sorts given his role in the case," Prichard said.

"Mr. Bringer's unique set of abilities has been instrumental to advances in the investigation," Denton said. "Not to mention he's saved the life of at least one of our agents on more than one occasion."

"Yes, let's talk about Mr. Bringer's abilities," Tevin agreed.

Click-click.

I cast a frown in Prichard's direction and saw the corners of her mouth upturn slightly in response.

"When did your abilities begin to surface, Mr. Bringer?" Tevin asked.

"Following my last cancer treatment before the explosion," I said.

My last *official* treatment, at least.

Click-click.

"And had you been expecting them to manifest by that time?" Prichard asked.

"I *expected* to be cured of brain cancer, Ms. Prichard," I replied. "I had no reason to expect anything more than the typical side effects associated with chemotherapy."

"So, you didn't know that the drug you were being given was experimental?" Tevin asked.

"Experimental? Yes," I said. "But at no time did anyone allude to—"

My mind suddenly drew a blank on how Maria had classified my abilities.

"Telekinetic abilities," Sanders supplemented.

I gave her an appreciative smile.

"I believe you read my mind, Agent Sanders," I quipped.

She smirked and a number of others chuckled.

Click-click.

"How amusing," Prichard flatly remarked. "Nevertheless, you failed to report your newfound abilities to Nuclegene Corporation. Why is that, Mr. Bringer?"

I paused to consider her question. Why indeed?

"At first, I was unsettled by what was happening to me," I said. "I thought I was hallucinating, in fact. Once I was convinced otherwise, I did contact someone with the company."

"And would that someone be Maria Edwards?" Prichard asked.

"Yes, it was Maria."

"The classified reports I read indicate you can move objects," Tevin said.

"That's correct," I confirmed.

Click-click.

"And are we to believe that you can also stop bullets?" Prichard asked.

"If it weren't for Mr. Bringer---" Sanders began.

Prichard cast her icy stare.

Click-click, click-click.

"I don't believe that we asked for your input yet, Agent Sanders," Prichard admonished.

I'd already had more than enough of Ms. Prichard and her condescending attitude, as well as her damned annoying pen.

I opened my right palm and her ink pen flew from her hand into mine like a magnet attracting iron.

There were a number of surprised gasps. As a matter of fact, the surprised expression on Prichard's face was priceless.

"You're a real menace with an ink pen, Ms. Prichard," I said in an even tone. "Would you care to stand up and shoot at me now so we can test my bullet-stopping ability?"

The room fell silent and I felt Sanders' hand touch my left arm lightly. Deputy Director Wainright caught my eye as he folded his arms across his chest.

His look was one of genuine amusement.

"That's *Special Agent* Prichard, Mr. Bringer," Prichard chastised. "And I'm not in the habit of having things taken from me like a child, so I suggest you relinquish my pen."

"Certainly," I replied with satisfaction and opened my palm.

The ink pen shot upward into the ceiling tile above us.

All eyes looked up at the ceiling while Sanders' hand

tightened around my left arm.

"Well, I'll be damned," Tevin muttered with near-fascination.

Sanders stifled a groan while Agent Denton barely contained his amusement.

Prichard glowered at me from across the table.

"You're a very disagreeable man, Mr. Bringer," Prichard said coldly. "That's a dangerous quality for someone with your abilities."

"Actually, *Special Agent* Prichard, I'm quite agreeable," I said. "That is, when I'm treated agreeably. And so far, I've only been dangerous to those trying to kill me, my family, or other innocent people."

"Very well-stated, Mr. Bringer," Wainright said, steepling his fingers before him in an almost meditative-looking fashion. "Yet another good reason why the Bureau has found merit in your continued assistance. How do you feel about that?"

I shrugged.

"Just pitchin' in where I can," I replied.

"You see, Prichard?" Wainright plainly asked. "The man sounds very agreeable to me. What say you, Tevin?"

Tevin's gaze pivoted between both Wainright and Prichard before settling upon me.

"I have no objections, though I'm primarily here as an observer to collect information for others," Tevin diplomatically stated.

All eyes turned to Special Agent Prichard, who still regarded me with unbridled contempt.

"Given that I have no authority to take Mr. Bringer into our custody at this time, I don't see that further dialogue with him would be productive to the CIA," Prichard said. "However, that assessment may be subject to change at some future point. And, of course, we will continue our own investigation into Continuance Corporation. It is, after all, a national security concern that extends beyond our country's borders."

Prichard rose from her seat, and her assistant, Russell Gasby, practically launched out of his seat to follow her.

"Good day, ladies and gentlemen," Prichard offered in a practiced tone. "Come, Gasby," she ordered, leading the way from the room.

After the conference room door shut behind them, Wainright looked up at the ceiling and casually observed, "I do believe the lady has forgotten her ink pen."

As far as I was concerned, Deputy Director Wainright was okay in my book.

* * *

Following additional discussion regarding the status of the investigation, the meeting concluded. Despite being NSA, Bob Tevin graciously thanked me for volunteering my services to the FBI and said he hoped to visit with me at some future time.

Following Tevin's departure, Deputy Director Wainright took me aside and shook my hand. "Bringer, you really have done the Bureau a service thus far. It's a shame I don't already have you on the payroll. But that's just between us, mind you. The circumstances are delicate and difficult at best at the moment," he offered.

There was an appeal to being on someone's payroll. I'd already been off work more than I should have been to maintain my meager lifestyle.

"Thanks," I said. "Nice to meet you, too, Deputy Director."

Wainright took Agent Denton in tow and headed down the hall toward the main office as Sanders cast me a cross look.

"What?" I asked.

"Really mature, Bringer," she admonished, looking up at the ceiling where the ink pen remainder lodged in the ceiling tile.

I held out my hand and the pen sprang into my open

palm. I smiled as I offered it to her.

She rolled her eyes at me.

"No, thanks," she said. "You absolutely *earned* that little souvenir."

She turned and walked out of the conference room, her heels clicking loudly on the hallway's tile floor.

"I can always use a spare pen," I said, pocketing it and walking after her.

"You do realize that you just made a formidable enemy back there," she challenged once I'd caught up to her.

We walked into the office and over to her desk where I commandeered her guest chair.

"Ha," I said. "I've met people like Prichard before. Those CIA types are way too full of themselves in my opinion. They don't exactly value the term *team*. Besides, Wainright didn't seem to mind so much."

"First of all, I'm confident that not everyone in the CIA is like Prichard. And second, Wainright and Prichard already have a storied history with each other," Sanders said as she logged onto her computer. "Rumor has it, they're always in competition with one another. However, you just came off like some egotistical wonder boy who's showing off his talents. Mark my words, you haven't heard the last of Prichard."

Mark my words? That seemed a bit theatrical to me.

"Don't you mean, I'll rue the day?" I teased.

She gave me a dark look. "Shut up, Bringer."

What had gotten into her all of the sudden?

"Look, you know as well as I do, I didn't show Prichard half of what I can do," I said. "And she can come knocking on my door anytime. I don't have any interest in the CIA. Besides, their agency's mission is based *outside* of the US, not *inside.*"

She exhaled with exasperation as her fingers pecked across her keyboard.

"So, what's next on our agenda?" I asked.

She stopped typing.

151

"*Our* agenda?"

I could tell by her expression I wasn't her favorite person at the moment.

"I'm going to file some reports based upon *our* latest exploits. Then I plan to research what we know in conjunction with additional clues being provided by our lab and forensic teams. And I'm still waiting on updates from the team investigating loose ends back in Chicago and the team following Justine Ziska in New York," she explained. "None of which involves throwing objects around the room, setting fires to buildings, or causing general havoc or mayhem."

"I get the impression you're annoyed with me right now," I said.

She glared back at me.

"I could help out with those reports," I offered.

"Not likely. Unlike you, they're official. Besides, I think we could both use a little time out, Bringer," she said. "Take a few hours off. Maybe go home and catch up on some sleep. The investigators are finished with your house, so it's all yours again. I'll call you later in the afternoon."

"Fine with me," I said with a shrug.

I glanced at my watch, realizing that it was already mid-morning.

I'd barely made it halfway across the room when Sanders called, "And, Bringer…try to stay out of trouble for just a couple of hours."

I winked and gave her a half-salute.

"I'll be a model citizen."

"I'll believe it when I see it," she retorted and returned her attention to her computer screen.

CHAPTER 15

Fortunately, the ever-appealing Agent Lana Collins offered to drop me off at my hotel to check out of my room and pick up my car. I confess, I found the attractive agent to be of more than just a passing interest. And I didn't have to be a mind reader to tell that she seemed at least mildly curious about me.

Still, I thanked her and let her drive away without either of us saying anything further.

I could only imagine how pleased Sanders would be with me if I'd actually asked Collins for a date; not that Sanders would mind on her own account.

Or would she?

Mere seconds of wily contemplation took place before banishing those thoughts into the farthest recesses of my mind. I had more pressing matters of immediate concern.

Upon returning to my house, I straightened up the overturned furniture and made some sense out of the chaos. The process was relatively benign enough for me to contemplate everything that had happened during the past few days.

Eventually, my thoughts gravitated back to Nevada and my newfound ability to hold fire at bay with my shielding talent. I recalled the fire that hovered above my hands following that feat, and it made me wonder if I could duplicate the effect.

I opened my palm and willed fire to appear.

Nothing.

Back to work.

Two hours later, the house was relatively passable. Meaning, of course, my sister would only give me hell, rather than faint straight away, if she saw my home's present state. Mom, on the other hand, might not have been so forgiving. Both had razzed me for years about my bachelor habits.

Housecleaning aside, and more importantly in my mind, I was no closer to duplicating the "hands on fire" event that had taken place in Henderson, Nevada.

That's when the closest person I had to a technical consultant came to mind.

Maria.

* * *

I called Maria before heading over to her house. She'd been home only a few hours, and I felt guilty for imposing upon her, but I couldn't help feeling that I needed to master as many useful abilities as possible for what might still lie ahead.

When I pulled into her driveway, I was happy to find a police car parked on the street with an officer in it. I showed him my FBI VIP badge, and he cleared my entry with another officer who was apparently inside the house.

I was happy the authorities were taking Maria's security seriously.

The imposing female corporal who met me at the front door looked as if she could easily hold her own.

As soon as I crossed the threshold, Maria practically leapt into my arms. Her slim body felt so frail that I held her like a china doll. The officer discreetly slipped outside, pulling the front door shut behind her.

"Thank you again, Logan," she breathed into my ear.

I closed my eyes and held her close, thankful that we'd found her in time. The warm, satisfied sensation flooding through me made me feel like the second-greatest man in the world.

When I opened my eyes, I saw Maria's daughter, Lauren, peeking at me from the hallway. I smiled at her and she grinned back at me before retreating down the hall. More than saving Maria, I'd reunited a mother with her children.

"I can never repay you for saving me," Maria whispered.

"No need. However, if it's not too much of an imposition, I *could* use your help," I softly suggested.

She pulled out of our embrace and looked into my eyes. Her telltale smirk and arched brow spoke volumes.

"I haven't known you long, but I already recognize that look. Let's go sit down on the couch, hero," she suggested.

She was the second person that week to call me hero. Even jokingly, I wished I'd felt more deserving of the moniker.

Within the hour, I'd explained everything that had happened, as well as described what I was trying to accomplish.

She held my right hand in both of hers and caressed my palm with her fingertips.

"Logan, I think you might be looking at this all wrong," she said. "You need to stop trying to mentally force everything into happening. Like with your shield ability, you just need to try and *let* it happen as you concentrate."

I clenched my jaw.

That's what I've been trying to do, for Christ's sake.

"You don't understand," I tried to explain. "It doesn't feel the same when I try making fire."

Her eyes narrowed. "Wait," she said.

I fell silent and watched as she stared at my hand, as if she was studying it.

"Did you try concentrating on the feeling that you felt in your hand?"

"The feeling?" I asked.

155

"Yes. You told me it was like a prickling feeling in your hands when you shielded the fire," she said.

I thought about it for a moment.

"Like a numbing sensation," I said.

She nodded.

I held my palm open before me and intently stared at it, trying to think about the fire and the feelings that I had felt.

"Close your eyes," she said.

"What?"

"Don't look," she explained. "Just concentrate on the feeling."

I closed my eyes and focused on recreating the feeling that I remembered from the experience. I felt a strange sensation go through my arm, so I continued to focus on thoughts of fire and the subsequent numbness.

After a few minutes, I was convinced that my hand was mimicking the desired sensations.

Maria softly ordered, "Logan, keep concentrating, but open your eyes."

I slowly opened my eyes and was surprised to see flames licking upward an inch or so above my palm. The numb, tingling sensations cascaded through my hand and across the skin of my palm.

"That's just flaming wonderful," I muttered as I rapidly waved my hand to extinguish the flames.

She giggled as I duplicated the flame-generating effort a number of times. It seemed to become easier with each instance.

"Now, Logan, find someplace private to practice some more," she said. "Just try not to burn down your house in the process."

I gratefully pressed a quick kiss on her cheek before leaving.

* * *

Though in jest, Maria had offered some excellent advice

to me about practicing, and I had a pretty good idea for a reasonable setting to hone both my current and newfound abilities. While Nevis Corners seemed to exist in a state of continued new construction, it was at a much smaller scale and slower pace than during its inception a decade prior. That left a number of dormant material supply sites just outside of town where large quantities of sand, dirt, and gravel had been staged.

As I stood in the midst of heaping mounds of dirt and sand that had compressed into dense berms over time, I appreciated the relative quiet around me. The sounds of birds and breezes whipping across untamed grasses and through nearby native oak, elm, and maple trees sounded uncannily soothing.

It was perfect.

I retrieved a litany of empty plastic containers from my car trunk, and mentally congratulated myself for recalling the drop-off location for the city's recycling program. Then I closed my eyes and concentrated on duplicating the flame generation technique that Maria had just helped me to manifest.

I marveled at the continuously licking flames and willed them to build. Fire rose as the tingling sensations in my palm increased and sweat beaded on my forehead.

Oh, this was *good*.

After I extinguished the flames, I held out my palm toward a nearby pile of gravel. A few pieces flew into my hand. I shifted all but one to my other hand and concentrated on projecting a single piece toward one of the plastic bottles placed before a nearby mound of compressed sand.

Though I missed the target, I came very close. I was reminded of how, as a youth, I'd practiced with the 22 caliber rifle that my father had given me for my birthday. My aim had been remarkably similar. Yet, by the time that I had enlisted in the army many years later, I'd been certified as a marksman.

I just needed more practice.

Within the hour, my aim had significantly improved. I rubbed my temples where a slight headache had started to build. While sipping from yet another chilled sports drink container that I'd brought in a cooler, I contemplated a host of concerns.

My sister and her family, as well as Maria, were safe for the moment, but I had no idea how long that might last as long as Continuance Corporation still had its sights on me.

Then there was the simple issue of income. My boss, Larry, had been really great about granting me another leave of absence. However, my savings was already running pretty thin, and in a few weeks I'd be hard-pressed to continue paying my bills.

And it wasn't as if the FBI had the intention of placing me on their payroll, either. Worse yet, who knew how long the bureau's investigations might take before Continuance's operations were able to be shut down, if ever.

I held my hand out for a nearby chunk of gravel mixed with concrete, and used my talent to cast it off into the distance toward an empty plastic jug.

It missed the target by mere inches, though the impact kicked up a considerable shower of sand.

"Where the hell is my life headed now?" I wondered aloud.

After high school, I'd thought that a career in the army was my destiny. Then after two tours in the Middle East, I determined that I'd had enough of that. That had been more about day-to-day survival and less about developing a career.

I'd hoped that completing my degree in business administration might open up opportunities in places like Nevis Corners. It seemed as if half the country was counting on these new corporate-sponsored cities as a panacea for stimulating employment in the country. Of course, few if any, of the politicians and government officials who'd enthusiastically supported the land reclamation legislation spoke openly about the growing urban blight in many old, traditional cities as they were abandoned by corporations for their shiny, new replacements.

It seemed to be the darkly-tinged yin and yang of progress; the elephant in the room that nobody wanted to talk about.

Then my cancer diagnosis came along, and life was merely about surviving again.

With my cancer in remission, I needed to get my life back on track again. The GI Bill had helped to support me financially while working part-time at the tag agency. In the end, it was probably my best bet to return to college and acquire a graduate degree. The GI Bill benefits would help to stabilize my financial situation, as well.

Regrettably, my recently acquired skill set was dubiously crafted for any traditional career opportunities.

I sardonically pondered if any nearby circuses were hiring new talent. Better yet, how did I feel about becoming an assassin or a heavy for some crime syndicate?

Then my thoughts drifted back to more immediate problems. For example, the continued safety of my family was of preeminent importance.

I finished my sports drink and returned to the task at hand. With lesser effort, I summoned flames into my palm and watched with fascination as they danced and flickered in the breeze.

"Great, I can be a human cigarette lighter."

For reasons I might never fully divine, I'd been given another chance at life, as well as gifts I could've barely conceived of only weeks prior. I needed to understand and hone my newfound abilities, as well as determine the best practical use for them.

A small cross breeze kicked up a momentary twister of sand that spiraled into a vortex and quickly dissipated. An idea struck, and after a few minutes of trial and error, I was able to manifest and build a sizable fire in my palm.

Concentrating until I felt the stirrings of a headache forming, I spun the flames into a circle. Then I tightened them into a smaller and smaller area, only to feel my entire body break out in a sweat as a throbbing headache painfully erupted. The circle of flames wound into a spherical shape as the spinning continued.

The sheer strain and concentration required for the effort was considerable and I was only able to maintain the effect for a series of seconds.

As I took a few minutes to rest and cool off, I stared at the line of plastic containers and bottles placed on the sandbar down range from me. A faint smile crossed my lips and I immediately felt like a kid with a strange, new toy.

Oh, this is going to be fun.

And just like the young boy with his new rifle had resolved so many years ago, it was once again time for me to practice.

* * *

I finished loading the remainder of the plastic containers, including some that were little more than melted semblances of their former selves, back into my car's trunk. It had been a few hours since I'd checked in with Agent Sanders, and I wanted to have time to take a shower back at my house before she summoned me back to the office.

Maybe she had simmered down a bit since I last saw her.

Traffic was scarce as I made my way down the county road back into town. My mind wandered to the sense of accomplishment I felt following my highly productive target practice session. Maybe knowing I'd been trying to be productive would help improve Sanders' dour mood somewhat.

I casually glanced into my rear-view mirror to see a dark sedan maintaining a paced distance behind me.

Come to think of it, I thought I'd seen a similar vehicle pass by as I had turned into the parking area back at the dormant material supply site. Though some might consider it paranoia, monitoring vehicles and structures was a habit that I'd gotten back into from being overseas. Being aware of your environment just might save your life sometime.

I unleashed the engine on my Dodge Avenger to put some distance between myself and the car behind me.

After a few minutes, I noticed the car appear in my rear-view mirror, though it maintained a relatively benign distance behind me.

Yep, sometimes it paid to monitor your surroundings.

Once again wantonly disregarding the state law against using a cell phone while driving, I dialed up Agent Sanders. Her voice was crisp when she answered.

"What's up, Bringer?" she asked. "And please don't tell me you've already managed to get into trouble."

"I'm so glad to hear you've got your sense of humor back, Sanders," I replied. "Listen, I'm out west of town heading back from a project, and I think I've got a tail. Have you got somebody out watching me?"

"Actually, that's not a bad idea," she conceded. "However, no, I don't. Describe the tail."

I looked in my rear-view mirror to confirm the vehicle was still shadowing me.

"Black sedan, but it's too far behind me to see how many might be inside," I said.

Sanders sighed.

"Well, Mr. Popularity, given all that's already happened with you today, it could be either CIA, NSA, or---"

"Continuance?" I interrupted.

"Possibly," she said in a flat voice. "Listen closely, Bringer. I'm sending Agent Foster to meet up with you and escort you back to the office. Where are you *exactly*?"

"I'm about three miles west of town on 165th, but I'm on my way to my house to take a shower, so have Foster meet me there," I said. "Listen, if some bozo wants to follow me around, that's their prerogative. However, they'd better be prepared for me not to like it."

"Wait just a minute, Bringer," Sanders warned. "Don't even think about confronting whoever it might be. Just hightail it back to your house and don't stop for anyone. And this time, no explosions, fires, or gunfights. Got it?"

"You're no fun," I said.

During the silent pause in our conversation, I spied a quick place to turn around.

"You're not listening to me, are you Bringer?"

I spotted a small courtesy stop ahead.

"You're the boss," I said and hung up the phone.

I accelerated to put some additional distance between myself and the car behind me. When I arrived at the courtesy stop, the parking lot hosted only an eighteen-wheeler.

I didn't stop, instead wheeling my car around to whip back out the exit heading back from where I'd come.

The black sedan appeared to slow as I approached it, so I accelerated, savoring the power of my Avenger's engine. I quickly discerned two men in the front seat, both wearing dark business suits and shades.

How cliché of them.

I rolled down my window, giving them a hard look as I passed. Their brake lights came on as I sped another hundred yards westward. Then I slammed on my brakes and deftly whipped my car back around to the east with a squeal of my tires.

I hit the accelerator and raced back toward the sedan.

The sedan's tail lights promptly went out and the vehicle began accelerating eastward as I gained on it. We quickly exceeded speeds over seventy miles per hour, though the sedan kept accelerating.

The lamebrains were probably feds of some variety.

Fortunately, traffic was light until we reached the outskirts of town, so nobody else on the road was threatened by our little melodrama. Still, it was nice to be on the giving, rather than the receiving, end for a change.

By the time we entered town proper, the sedan sped through a red light to try and lose me and turned onto a northbound side street. However, I stopped at the traffic light and let them go.

Jerks.

I'd become a little too popular for my own preference. Then I frowned and wondered if they'd observed me practicing back at the construction materials site.

Can't a guy even practice his magic tricks in peace?

Still, I realized I needed to be a hell of a lot more careful in the future.

CHAPTER 16

By the time I made it home, there were two government-style sedans parked in my driveway. Both Sanders and Foster were leaning against one of the cars with their arms folded before them. They looked like parents who were anxiously waiting for their teenager to show up well after curfew.

I pulled in front of my house and got out as if nothing had happened.

"A welcoming committee? Hey, thanks for caring and all," I chimed.

Foster shook his head with an amused expression, even as he dialed someone on his cell phone and walked out onto the edge of the driveway to look down the street from the direction I'd come.

Meanwhile, Sanders waited for me to approach her before she pushed herself away from the car.

"You sure took your sweet time getting here," she admonished.

"It's great to see you too, Sanders," I quipped as I continued walking to my front door.

"Well?" she asked as I unlocked the door and strode into my living room.

"My new friends weren't very sociable," I said. "They sped off soon after we entered the city limits."

She frowned at me as I stripped off my shirt and walked into the hallway.

"That's it?" she demanded. "And just where are you going?"

I turned to see her watching me with more than an appraising expression, and I grinned back at her. She quickly diverted her gaze to look out my living room window.

"Me? I'm gonna' take a shower, partner," I said. "Then you can fill me in on what I may have missed while I was gone."

As I entered my bedroom, I heard her exclaim, "Rather *you're* going to tell *me* what you were doing out west of town. And we're *not* partners, Bringer."

"Whatever you say, partner," I quipped, only to hear her growl as I closed my bedroom door.

By the time I finished showering and changing into fresh clothes, Agent Foster had left to conduct a field interview related to the investigation. Meanwhile, Agent Sanders was seated at my dining room table scribbling on a notepad while conversing with someone on her cell phone.

"...need to follow up on the details later. For now, I recommend around the clock protection until further notice. Yes, I'll ask my supervisor to sign off on the official request this afternoon and then fax it over to your office no later than this evening. Thank you," she said.

I retrieved a plastic jug of sports drink from the refrigerator.

"Naturally, the federal government still faxes things," I teased. "Haven't you heard of scanning and emailing attachments? Hell, I was a ground-pounder and I know how to do that."

"Funny. I thought that you had drowned in there. Honestly, for a macho guy, you take longer than a woman," she said.

"Hey, after years deployed in Godforsaken deserts, I tend to enjoy my showers more," I said, then took a long swig from my glass.

166

"Whatever. And you're not even going to offer me something to drink?" she prodded. "I think I've finally pierced your gentlemanly facade, Bringer."

"Well, my apologies, Ms. Sanders," I offered with a grand gesture of my arm. "Would madam care for something to drink?"

"No, thanks," she replied offhandedly.

I cast her a disparaging look but her attention had already shifted to the notepad before her.

"I just got off the phone with a captain at the Des Moines PD," she began.

I looked up, recognizing that's where my parents lived, which was also where Lexi and her family were staying.

"What's happening in Des Moines?" I asked in a dark tone.

Sanders looked up at me with a surprised expression, and reassured me, "Everything's fine. I'm increasing the security precautions for your family, that's all."

"Oh."

I relaxed and finished my drink in a couple of quick swigs.

"While you were off on your own little mission today, I was busy going over the latest update from Chicago," she began.

"Did they find out what happened to our shooter?" I asked.

"Somewhat."

I poured another glass of Gatorade.

"I was wondering why he hadn't shown up to disrupt our Nevada raid," I said.

"As was I," she said. "It turns out that our shooter may have been more injured than we thought. The Chicago team placed him at a rundown hotel on the south side. Based upon some grainy hotel video, he'd departed the hotel in haste, and tried to firebomb the room to destroy evidence. Lucky for us, the timer malfunctioned and the device was discovered by a maid. There were bloody hotel towels and residue on the floor and sink area. Forensics believes that our suspect lost quite a bit of blood, suggesting that either one of our rounds managed to wound him or you tossing him through the air caused some injuries. Either way, it bodes well for us if his activities are curtailed while we're trying to find him."

"He's a professional," I said. "If he doesn't want to be found, we won't find him easily."

"Maybe not," Sanders said. "Still, I'd rather he be on the run versus us always being one step behind trying to keep up with him."

"True," I agreed. "So, what's next?"

"Actually, I was considering that while you were primping," she said with a smug expression.

I started to counter with something sarcastic but the doorbell interrupted my train of thought. As I walked into the living room, I heard Sander's chair scoot, and I looked back to see her stand up with her hand approaching her hip.

"Assassins don't generally ring the doorbell," I said.

"And you haven't seen as many movies as I have," she countered. "Try to stand out of my line of fire."

I gazed through the peephole in my door.

"Well, he's a familiar face," I said.

I opened the front door to find my front porch occupied by no less than four people. Clive Bernard looked smart in his tailored suit, and he had a satisfied looking expression on his face. Behind him stood his executive assistant, Sandra Yalesin, who was grasping a small leather documents satchel. Beside her stood two suit-clad gentlemen bearing guarded expressions. Given that one of the men was Scott, his heavy, I anticipated the other was another one of Bernard's corporate bodyguards.

"Good afternoon, Mr. Bringer," Bernard offered as he reached out to shake my hand. "I hope you won't mind me dropping by unannounced. Is this a good time for us to chat?"

"That depends," Sanders suspiciously replied before I could respond.

Bernard piqued my curiosity, so I shook his outstretched hand and stood aside for him to enter.

"Certainly, come in," I said.

Bernard and Yalesin entered while Scott and his partner remained outside. As I scanned my living room, I realized how chaotic the condition of my house still was. I'm sure it looked like I was a real slob. Still, it wasn't as if I'd planned to entertain visitors given all that had happened recently.

I gestured to the kitchen.

"Let's sit at the table," I suggested. "You'll have to pardon my home's appearance; like me, it's been through quite a bit recently. Can I offer you something to drink? I'm afraid all I have is a variety of sports drinks, water, and maybe some cola."

"Nothing for us, thank you," Bernard replied as he and Yalesin seated themselves at the table.

Before Sanders sat down, Bernard queried, "I wonder if we might converse with you in private, Mr. Bringer?"

"I'm afraid Mr. Bringer and I can't comment on topics related to the investigation," Sanders warned.

"I can assure you, Agent Sanders, my business with Mr. Bringer has little to do with your immediate investigation."

I exchanged looks with Sanders, and she shrugged.

"I have an errand to run," Sanders said. "I'll pick up some sandwiches for us and be back in an hour or so."

As she recovered her notepad from the table, I reached for my wallet.

"I think I can afford sandwiches," Sanders said. "Besides, I've seen your bank account balance."

My jaw clenched. It really wasn't anybody else's business how lean my financial condition was.

Taking the high road from issuing my displeasure, I said, "I'll have---"

"I've seen you eat, Bringer," she interrupted.

"Great. Think mustard," I said as she walked to the front door.

"Think *free*," Sanders countered with a smirk, glancing

back at me before she closed the front door behind her.

That lady could dish it out better than anyone I'd met recently. I returned to sit at the table, and noticed that Ms. Yalesin was struggling to maintain a reserved expression as she sorted through a folder of paperwork before her.

Thankfully, Bernard was all business.

"I've noticed some of your recent exploits on the news recently," he began.

"It's been a busy week," I said.

"I'm sure it has. And I'm willing to venture that, given your busy schedule, you haven't had an opportunity to earn a living recently."

I stared Bernard straight in the face, not liking his choice of topic. However, I had to admit that my protracted leave of absence was heavily impacting my financial stability. During my initial cancer treatments, I'd only barely been able to afford my utilities and house payment, much less mounting medical bills.

Fortunately, I could continue to pay on medical bills over a seemingly unlimited period time without penalty of interest.

That's not to say I looked forward to the next forty years of monthly installments.

"I have to wonder why you've taken such a keen interest in my income, Mr. Bernard," I said with an edge to my voice.

"Please forgive my directness, Mr. Bringer. I meant no offense," he offered. "Rather, I've been given approval by our company's owner, Mr. Nevis Wallace, to extend an offer of employment to you. Nuclegene Corporation could use someone like you in their ranks."

I remained silent as I studied his sober-looking features.

"Please permit me to be frank, Mr. Bringer. Nuclegene has invested a great deal of time, money, and research into treating your brain cancer. The fact that we've been successful in curing your cancer not only brings a great deal of pride to us, but encourages us to continue our research," Bernard continued. "Our hope is that by studying your successful experience, we can refine and improve our efforts, thereby helping so many other cancer patients just like you."

I noticed that any mention of my special abilities was notably absent.

"So, you want to hire me to become a human guinea pig so you can create more people like me?" I asked.

Bernard's hand immediately rose in a gesture of protest.

"Hardly, Mr. Bringer. I mean nothing of the sort," he said. "Rather, as a manifestation from your cancer treatments, you embody recently-acquired talents and skills that our company would find very marketable. In addition to the non-invasive opportunity to study your physiology and our medication's unusual side-effects, your services could help our company secure significant contractual opportunities with key government agencies."

I quietly considered what he'd said as I nursed my sports drink. While it was true that my efforts at college were intended to help me secure a position with a prominent company, my present circumstances provided me an edge that hadn't been a part of my initial plan. If not for my body's manifested talents, I would likely have merited little more than a passing glance from either Bernard or the company; just another job applicant vying for limited position openings.

Wasn't it reasonable for me to take advantage of what my newfound skills had afforded me?

Then another thought crossed my mind; something Bernard had said, or rather, hadn't said.

"Precisely, what sort of marketable opportunities do I provide to Nuclegene?" I asked. "Circus act qualifications aside, of course."

Bernard's teal eyes discreetly peered at Ms. Yalesin, who was closely observing her supervisor while she tapped on an iPad before her.

"You and Agent Sanders seem to have developed an interesting rapport. How do you like working with the FBI, Mr. Bringer?" he asked.

His question came out of left field and stopped my

mental train as it coasted in its tracks, though whether it was due more to his reference of Agent Sanders or to working with the FBI, I wasn't certain.

"Well, it's certainly better than being a key suspect in their investigations," I replied.

He appeared reflective for a moment.

"I believe we can both agree upon that simple truth," he said. "What would you say if I told you that you could continue working with the FBI on a continued basis while also being paid for your time?"

Bernard had definitely earned my complete attention.

"Your company can actually facilitate that?" I asked. "How, and more importantly, why?"

"What I'm about to discuss with you is not a matter of, or for, public knowledge. I must therefore ask for your confidence before we proceed further," he insisted.

"Does your request include the FBI?" I asked.

Based upon the surprised expression on his face, the question must've caught him slightly off guard.

"Certainly, if you were to accept our offer, the FBI would know soon enough," Bernard temporized. "For now, let's keep the shared circle of information minimal, shall we?"

That seemed reasonable enough. I nodded my assent.

"It's hardly a secret that, in this new era of government-corporate partnerships, many companies vie for lucrative government contracts," Bernard explained. "To my knowledge, you're the only person in America with your kind of unique talents and skills. That makes you highly in demand to government entities who may desire the use of those skills."

"Why wouldn't they simply hire me themselves?" I asked.

Bernard adopted a sly expression.

"I think you'll find that government entities tend to become mired in their own bureaucracies concerning their employees, policies, and procedures," he said. "Add to that, those same agencies are always under the scrutiny of the press and other public advocacy groups, including labor unions."

I recalled similar challenges from my days in the army. Despite being a military organization, it had been rife with both politics and bureaucracy. That's never a good combination when lives were in the balance on a minute-by-minute basis deep within enemy territory. It had been one of the key reasons I elected to end my military career so early.

"Private contractors have the ability to operate outside such bureaucracies," he continued. "We streamline the process and achieve maximum results over greatly-reduced time periods."

Something registered in my mind with complete clarity.

"And if contractors screw up, government entities have plausible deniability," I suggested.

Bernard appeared pleased.

"Precisely, Mr. Bringer," he said. "However, I like to frame it that private companies save the taxpayers from unnecessary overhead expenditures such as benefits and entitlements, while also achieving government goals and objectives by leveraging private sector efficiencies. In the end, such efforts help to stimulate the economy with job opportunities for the general public."

It was the whole Land Reclamation and Investment in America Act spiel all over again. Once that message was stated and restated long enough, people began to believe it, and then buy into it.

"That's all very enlightening, Mr. Bernard," I said. "But you still haven't explained how your company is in such an ideal position to offer my services to the FBI."

Bernard absently tapped two fingertips against his lips as he stared back at me.

"Let's just say that our company has access to influential government leaders who are in a position to favor what we have to offer," he replied.

I couldn't help but wonder how far up the ladder such influences extended, though I seriously doubted that Bernard was about to provide that level of information to me.

"Aren't you afraid of how unusual it might look if your company was offering contractual services to the FBI at a time when the agency is investigating terrorist activities surrounding your company's operations?" I asked.

I felt proud over having divined that consideration. After all, Mom and Dad hadn't raised an idiot.

"That might be true, except that Nuclegene Corporation stands as one of the *victims* of a terrorist plot," Bernard said. "If anything, it's highly patriotic that we would offer our company's services to the nation at such a challenging time. And to what better agency than the FBI?"

I had to hand it to Bernard; it appeared that he and his company had already scrutinized key publicity angles on the topic.

"Why don't you tell me a little bit more about a proposed salary and benefits," I said. "Then I'll think about it and get back to you."

As Ms. Yalesin effortlessly produced a number of documents for me to peruse, Bernard's expression transformed to that of someone who'd just found out he'd won the lottery.

CHAPTER 17

Bernard and Yalesin had already left my house by the time Sanders returned with our sandwiches. She'd been as surprised as I'd been once I confided to her about the discussion I'd just finished with Bernard.

"May I ask what they offered you?" Sanders asked.

I was quite happy to share that information with her.

Her eyes nearly bulged from her head. "Holy crap, Bringer!" she exclaimed. "I don't know anyone in the bureau making that kind of money. Well, except perhaps Deputy Director Wainright's boss, though I'm not even certain of that."

It was true the proposed salary was at least ten times more than I could've hoped from even a competitive entry-level executive salary. Suddenly, the reality of paying off my medical bills took on a much shorter timeframe.

All I had to do was agree to the terms and all that went with it.

"Bernard presented me with a host of intriguing possibilities," I said. "However, I wonder if there were things that he may have left unsaid that might trouble me."

"Yeah? Like what?" she asked.

"I don't know precisely," I said with a frown. "It just seems there's frequently strings attached to a lot of really good deals."

"I admit, it does sound a bit too good to be true," Sanders said. "However, if you decided to take him up on his offer, you can buy our sandwiches from now on."

I grinned, unwrapping the turkey breast sandwich she'd placed before me.

"Thanks," I said. "Hey, you even remembered the mustard."

She cast me a smirk that appeared particularly alluring on her.

"I *am* an FBI agent, after all."

As we ate, I briefly recounted my run-in with the unknown men earlier that afternoon, as well as the nature of my practice session outside of the city limits.

"I should commend you for finding some place relatively out of sight and out of harm's way to others for you to practice, I suppose," Sanders said.

Then we talked about the state of the investigation.

"Where do we go from here?" I asked.

"Until we get more leads on our renegade shooter or receive more clues as to the identity of the mysterious woman that Maria alluded to, we're sort of dead in the water. We could interview Justine Ziska in New York, though we're still gathering intelligence on her."

"So, what about Folker?" I asked.

"Or Volker," Sanders said with a shrug. "Either way, we have nothing definitive to go on at this point."

Once we finished eating, Sanders rose from the table.

"Going back to the office?" I asked.

"Nah, too tired," she said.

She stretched her arms above her head, and I took a moment to appreciate her slender physique and the way that her fitted shirt clung to her. I found her to be a very attractive woman. Of particular interest, she had rather kissable-looking lips.

"What?" she asked.

"Me? Nothing," I said evasively.

Uh-oh, dangerous territory, Bringer.

She briefly frowned at me as she slipped her suit jacket back on.

"Why don't you take the day off tomorrow," she suggested. "There's no need to have you sitting around the office when there's nothing for you to do. I'll call you if something comes up."

"Sure, thanks," I said as I followed her to the front door.

To my surprise, the sun had already set. Time had definitely flown since that afternoon.

Sanders turned back to me as she stepped onto the front porch. Her hazel eyes glistened back at me in the glow of the porch light.

"I have to admit that, despite the dire circumstances surrounding this case, it's been great working with you, Bringer," she offered. "I feel bad that the bureau's leveraging your abilities for free. And if you do choose to take the job with Nuclegene, maybe it can be a win-win situation for us both."

I frowned, not really certain if there were multiple layers to her last statement. However, I had to admit the idea of spending more time around her was certainly appealing; not to mention the ability to secure an enviable level of income.

"Thanks," I said. "I feel much the same way, Sanders."

After she left, I contemplated the generous offer that Bernard had extended to me. It had to have been an indication of how badly Nuclegene wanted to secure my services, including assisting their research and development division in perfecting the formula that had given me my abilities.

Certainly, the idea that many more people might be cured of their cancer was a hopeful thought. However, I had to wonder if the world was better off with many more people wandering around with my level of abilities.

Worse yet, what if their treatments were able to manifest even greater abilities than my own? How might the world be shaped by the inclusion of scores of people like me, or more powerful than me?

I wasn't sure that I liked those prospects very much. It seemed to me that the world was already more than volatile enough as it was.

* * *

I woke abruptly to the sound of my doorbell ringing. I staggered from the bed, glancing at the clock as I passed the dresser.

It was barely seven-thirty in the morning.

"Just great," I muttered while looking through the peephole in my front door.

The image of Agent Sanders standing there made me groan. I slowly opened the front door.

"I thought you said I had the day off, Sanders," I said sleepily.

Her brow arched as she regarded me standing before her wearing only army green sweatpants. I folded my arms before my bare chest and leaned against the front doorjamb.

Her expression was momentarily wistful, but quickly reverted back to her business-like demeanor as she cleared her throat. Having regained her composure, she squeezed past me to enter.

"Aren't you up yet? I thought you were in the army?" she half-chastised, half-teased.

"To what do I owe this pleasure?" I asked before issuing a wide-mouthed yawn.

She rolled her eyes at me in disgust.

"Do you happen to recall that I'm helping you with your daily whatever-it-is vitamin shot until I had time to show you how to do it?"

Oh, yeah.

I swept past her into the kitchen and retrieved a pre-measured syringe of vitamin solution from the refrigerator. She snatched it from my hand, and like an old pro, removed the cap by grasping it between her teeth as she rubbed my arm where the injection was to be made.

"You could always show me how to do this right now, you know," I prompted.

"No time this morning," she said. "Besides, if I don't show you properly, you'll just end up with air bubbles in your veins."

She popped the needle into my arm and deftly injected the solution. The entire process took only a matter of seconds.

"Here," she said, handing the empty syringe back to me.

Then she turned and headed straight for the front door.

"Same time tomorrow morning?" I asked. "Hey, maybe next time I'll have coffee ready for you," I teased.

"Shut up, Bringer," she growled.

I watched her drive away with a grin.

Then it was just me and my somewhat of a mess house, which made me feel both helpless and irritable. I needed action, not hurry-up-and-wait.

But what else could I do at the moment?

I cast a withering look around the inside of my house. Despite my recent endeavors, it was still a wreck. But who the hell cared about housecleaning when there were thugs out there somewhere plotting who-knows-what?

"Here we go again. Situation normal, all fucked up."

Then inspiration struck in the form of someone else's home.

My sister's.

I shaved, got dressed, and grabbed a pair of heavy gloves from the garage as I headed for my car.

* * *

By the time I arrived at my sister's house, I realized it was a good thing I considered stopping by. She and Kevin were already onsite sifting through the rubble.

They both waved at me as I pulled in front of their wreck of a home. True to his word, my best friend, Travis, had seen to some of the cleanup and recovery. A couple of large portable storage containers were located on the property, one of which Kevin was sorting through.

Lexi met me at the car and gave me a big hug. In truth, I probably needed it as much as she did.

"Hey, Sis," I said. "What're you doing here?"

She parted from our hug and shrugged.

"Kevin and I just couldn't stay at Mom and Dad's for much longer," she said. "It was driving us crazy! So, we left the kids with them and just arrived back in town last night. I planned to call you later today, once we had a chance to go through what's left here."

There were already signs of a teardown taking place. At least their insurance company was on top of things.

"Yeah, well, it's still dangerous for you to be here," I said, though I'd noticed a police car parked in front of a neighbor's property across the street when I pulled up.

She sighed.

"About that," she said sharply. "We've been watching the news reports, and we're pretty sure you were in some of the footage. I tried texting you a couple of times, but you ignored them. What's with all the mystery, and when are you planning to tell us what the hell's going on?"

I nearly winced from her tone. Drill sergeants had nothing on my sister.

Still, she had a point.

I led her over to where Kevin stood in the driveway.

"All right. What I'm about to tell you stays between us, got it? Not even Mom and Dad can know about this yet."

They both nodded.

I took a deep breath.

"Let's walk over to a safer portion of your house," I said. "I need to show you something."

They followed me inside, and then I opened Pandora's Box for them.

"Holy shit," Lexi muttered wide-eyed as I handed her the small ruined picture that had formerly been hanging on the wall of their smoke-damaged study.

My skills with grabbing nearby objects had definitely improved over the past week or so.

"Where in hell did you learn to do that?" Kevin demanded, still sporting a shocked expression on his face.

Lexi stared at me expectantly.

"It all goes back to Nuclegene and those cancer treatments that I'd been taking," I said.

After I'd gone over most everything in detail, both of them were rather speechless. However, I left out the part about the Nuclegene job offer for the time being.

"So, it's true then," Lexi finally said. "That guy they showed on the video clip in Chicago…you were the one who flung him into the air?"

I shrugged.

"It wasn't my finest work to date, but yeah," I said. "We're still trying to find the guy. The sooner the better, in fact. He's an assassin of some kind."

A restless feeling coursed through me as I realized that I really needed to be out trying to find that bastard.

Still, I had to wait for Sanders before I could do much.

Kevin checked his watch.

"Aren't you going to the memorial service, Logan?" he asked.

I frowned.

"Memorial service? What memorial service?"

Lexi gave me a hopeless-looking expression. "You really don't watch as much TV as I thought, do you, dear brother?"

"Easy there. I've been a little preoccupied, if you hadn't noticed," I said.

"Hey, don't get snippy," she teased.

How she managed to maintain such good humor while standing in the middle of her burned house, I'll never know.

"They've scheduled a public memorial service downtown for the Wallace Building victims for later this afternoon. The US President, senators, and congressmen are expected to be there, as well as a bunch of state officials. I'm kind of surprised nobody told you about it," Kevin said.

It caught me a little off-guard, as well.

"Well, I guess I'd better go change clothes then," I said. "You two stay close to those police officers and I'll call you later."

* * *

When I called Agent Sanders, she said she knew about the memorial service but hadn't given it a thought as she'd been squarely focused on the investigation at hand. Naturally, I shared her focus.

However, she was unusually willing to meet me downtown when I told her my intention to be there for it.

"Why not watch it on TV?" she asked.

"I'm sort of curious to see who might show up, if you know what I mean."

Her silence over the phone spoke volumes.

"I'll meet you. Call me once you're down there," she said, and abruptly hung up.

Parking was a nightmare, and I had to walk nearly a mile just to get near the assemblage. To say the police presence was high was an understatement. I spotted no fewer than a dozen snipers on rooftops downtown.

The event was scheduled to take place at the downtown convention center, though seating was at a premium, so large screens had been set up around the city where people could gather and view the event live. Fortunately, it was a relatively nice day, so at least the weather was cooperating.

I met Sanders and Agent Denton, who looked appropriately dressed in business suits, standing outside of a small deli, not far from the convention center. Most of the downtown restaurants were filled with customers wanting to sit and watch the memorial service.

"Let's go," Denton quickly instructed, leading the way across the street toward the convention center.

"You can get us in there?" I asked.

"Right now, with this investigation in our lap, I can probably get you places you've never thought possible," Denton said.

I had to admit I was impressed.

We practically whisked through security by comparison to the other invited guests and citizens who were fortunate enough to secure seating, though it still meant a number of pat-downs and verifications of our credentials.

Even then, we couldn't get anywhere near the President's reserved areas within the building.

Still, we managed to procure some metal foldout chairs that were hastily placed in a viewing area near a Secret Service gathering point on the second level.

Denton and Sanders both produced small pairs of binoculars they'd been carrying and started scanning the faces in the crowd.

"What are you two looking for?" I asked, feeling somewhat inadequate without my own form of vision enhancement.

"*We're* looking for anything that looks suspicious," Sanders said. "*You're* supposed to be watching the event. But let us know if you happen to pick up on anything useful."

I swallowed hard at the prospect of opening my mind to thousands of prospective voices in my head. I imagined my head exploding over the attempt.

Instead, I tried to concentrate on someone near me, hoping to exclude those close by.

An elderly woman seated a dozen feet from me appeared as a good likely test subject.

Almost immediately, I was assailed by a cacophony of voices, which forced my hands to the sides of my head as I reeled in my seat.

"You okay?" Sanders immediately asked.

"Yeah, just trying something here," I said, recovering my wits.

I felt her breath against my ear as she whispered, "Logan, don't kill yourself, okay? If you can't, you can't."

I turned to stare into her eyes, our noses nearly touching for a second, and noted the sincerity and concern reflected.

"Thanks," I said, fully appreciating both her gesture and her proximity to me.

She blinked and quickly backed away from me and returned to scanning the crowd with her binoculars.

I quickly lost track of how many dignitaries took the podium, each conveying their regrets, shock, and determination not to allow the perpetrators to go unpunished. In their own way, each also spoke of the importance of family and loved ones, of the tragic and abrupt loss that had occurred, and of the need for a time of reflection and healing.

I couldn't deny degrees of validity or appropriateness for what each of the event's speakers had said; I shared each of those feelings at some level myself. However, I mostly felt a pervasive sense of drive to find and stop anyone associated with the explosion that might also have an agenda that threatened my family.

Or Maria and her family.

Or Megan Sanders.

Or me.

But there was another underlying feeling within me, as well; a need that was both motivational and dark.

Retribution.

As I scanned the litany of faces of special guests and dignitaries on the stage, I noticed one in particular; someone who I'd not seen in a number of years.

My old friend and former member of my fire team in Afghanistan sat between two other politicians.

Paul Criswell, the moderate-minded Democratic congressman from New York.

What's he doing here?

I was surprised to see him in the audience, not being part of the contingent representing Iowa. In fact, he sat beside another non-Iowan, Republican Senator Benjamin Conway of Utah.

That was definitely an odd pairing.

I had little time to contemplate the matter further as the president was introduced and all eyes and ears focused upon him.

When President Graydon spoke, he captivated the audience with his charming southern drawl, dripping with empathy. Beau Graydon, an ultra-conservative Republican and former senator from South Carolina, was one of the founders and chief proponents of the Land Reclamation and Investment in America Act nearly a decade ago while serving in the senate; the catalyst for Nevis Corners and other corporate cities like it. The historic bill had served as his personal golden ticket into the White House a couple of years ago; swept into office amidst the fervor and promise of a new Golden Age in our economy. He, above many, likely took the terrorist attack in Nevis Corners as a personal affront.

In fact, a portion of his speech suggested as much.

"Americans are a talented, industrious people; born of grit and determination, as well as compassion. We're prone to neither wrath nor fury," he said.

"However, when confronted with such a hateful crime as terrorism, Americans gird themselves in their faith and beliefs, ever vigilant against evil powers which lash out against all that we hold sacred; things such as faith, family, and the enduring spirit of freedom that were born of centuries ago."

"When I look upon the ashes of the Wallace Building and see the faces of so many whose loved ones were ripped from their arms, I feel love and sympathy for the victims and their families. Yet, I also feel a determination that no border, or power, or barrier can withstand; a resolve that such hateful crimes will not go unanswered. I can only promise to my fellow Americans that justice will ultimately be done," he said.

Following subdued clapping, the president returned to the gentler messages of support and consolation. However, the air felt charged with something quiet and ominous; like calm before a storm.

Then again, maybe it more closely reflected the emotions

within me.

The event wrapped up promptly after the president spoke. He quickly exited the building, along with a small army of Secret Service personnel, leaving the rest of us to assert order amidst the waves of people lining up to exit. Denton, Sanders, and I barely managed to negotiate our way to the reserved security area, in fact.

As we exited the center, I spied a glimpse of Paul Criswell as he accompanied a number of fellow politicians out of the building.

"Paul!" I yelled, trying and get his attention.

He looked my direction and nodded, but then turned and made his way in the opposite direction.

Really?

After he'd gone to the trouble to call my mother to ask about me, he couldn't even spare a moment to say hello?

Yes, he was an important congressman and it was a crazy sort of day, but I couldn't help feeling as if he'd just disregarded me rather casually.

It kinda' pissed me off, actually.

"What's wrong?" Sanders asked as she pressed against my shoulder while negotiating the crowd.

"Nothing," I said. "Just saw somebody I used to know."

CHAPTER 18

Denton and Sanders returned to the office, so I got in the car and headed home. In truth, I still had a mild headache from my earlier attempts at overhearing people's thoughts on such a grand scale.

When my cell phone rang, I'd just plopped down onto the couch with a cold glass of Gatorade and turned on the TV.

I noted the caller ID and frowned.

It was an elusive person from my past; someone I was still slightly annoyed with at the moment.

"Hello? Bringer speaking," I said in a practiced tone.

"Hi, Logan. It's Paul Criswell."

"Hi, Paul. So nice of you to call," I said with an edge to my voice.

"Yeah, listen, Bringer, sorry we didn't get a chance to talk earlier today," he said. "It was a big to-do and rather tightly scripted; heavy with public expectations and key politicians to shake hands with and elbows to rub. You understand, right?"

"Sure, Paul," I said.

Actually, his social circles and mine were worlds apart since we both left the Army.

"Logan, I know this is pretty short notice and it's been

long time since we've talked, but I'd appreciate it if you and I could meet privately this evening," he said.

Aside from perhaps calling my sister, my night was destined for just me and the television, so how could I resist?

"Sure," I said. "When and where?"

"How about an hour from now," he said. "Meet me at the downtown central park next to the city founders' display."

"Okay. Got it."

"And, Logan, it's important that you come alone," he cautioned. "Nobody but my administrative aide and I know we're meeting, and I'd like to keep this on the QT, if you don't mind."

"Got it, Paul," I said. "See you tonight."

"Thanks," he said before our connection ceased.

Just great. Clandestine meetings with politicians. Nothing ever goes wrong when those happen, right?

I half-considered calling Sanders, but then thought better of it. She probably would've insisted on coming along, which was exactly what Paul had asked me not to do.

Within the hour, I stood next to the commemorative tribute to the primary corporate players behind the founding of Nevis Corners. The sun had already set by the time that I'd arrived, leaving the park dimly lit beneath sporadic lampposts.

I stared at the elaborate stone and marble structure; an imposing centerpiece near the middle of the picturesque park. It was a huge, gaudy-looking example of corporate self-aggrandizement. The rock base was comprised of large stone chunks from local quarries, as well as large marble slabs serving as the backdrop for the etchings. Copper and some steel accented part of the trim.

In totality, it was a solid reminder that this was a corporate city; a shining beacon of capitalism.

Of course, in my mind, there wasn't anything wrong with capitalism. But, like most anything, there had to be limits; and right now, in our place and time, corporations were the irresistible giants on Earth.

Or, at least, in America they were.

The partnership between one major contributing corporation, Corners Industries, and multi-billionaire American investor, Nevis Wallace, had been the catalyst for the sprawling city that I now called home.

What was the world coming to when our government was willing to parcel out stretches of privately owned land just to appease monolithic corporations? Was it really just a modern replaying of the Carnegie's and the Vanderbilt's all over again?

"Thanks for meeting me, Logan," came a voice to my right.

I started, silently berating myself for allowing my guard to drop and my mind to wander. That would've never happened back in the prime of my army days.

You're getting lazy, Bringer.

"Hi, Paul," I said, exchanging a handshake and quick fraternal half-hug with my distant friend and former sergeant who'd saved my life so many years ago.

"How are Denise and the kids?" I asked.

"Doing great, thanks," he replied.

Paul's welcoming smile turned serious, and I couldn't help but wonder why we were meeting so discreetly.

He looked up at the corporate display next to us.

"It seems like a lifetime ago since cities like Nevis Corners sprang up across this country," he said. "So many hopes and dreams, all waiting to come to fruition and become the catalyst for another hundred years of economic prosperity."

I frowned.

"You met me out here on a cool night to wax nostalgia over the Land Reclamation and Investment in America Act?" I asked. "Hell, we could've had a cold beer in a nice warm bar for that."

He chuckled.

"Same old, Bringer," he teased. "Give it to me straight and cut the bullshit."

I shook my head with a good-natured expression. Paul

had always been the visionary one with big dreams in our group.

"Truthfully, I like that beer idea," he agreed.

"Been a long time since we just talked," I said, changing the subject. "Been even longer since our days back overseas."

He nodded and sighed.

"A long time," he agreed. "Now, here we are again."

"Why is that, exactly, Paul?"

He paused, glancing up at the stone and marble display, and then turned his back to it to face me.

"I'm really glad your cancer treatments were successful," he offered. "Your mom was pretty broken up when the traditional chemotherapy and radiation treatments failed."

I thought back to those days, and the sad truth was that I'd been ready to say goodbye to everyone. Those were rough days, and it about killed me to see my parents and sister in such emotional pain.

Those were dark days.

"Thanks. I was really lucky," I said.

The faces of my fellow cancer patients who'd lost their lives in the Wallace Building explosion flashed through my mind.

Who knew how many of them might've been cured as well, given time?

"Mom really appreciated your phone calls, Paul," I said.

"Your mother's an amazing lady," he agreed. "I still remember the phone call when she asked if there was anything that I could do to help get you into the Nuclegene trials. I was happy to help."

I looked up sharply and stared into Paul's eyes.

"You didn't know?" he asked incredulously.

"No," I said. "Mom told me that she'd seen some article in a medical journal that Nuclegene was holding trials for a new form of chemotherapy. She directed me to their website to apply for the program, but she never mentioned calling you."

He appeared just as surprised as I felt, so I didn't doubt

his word. Still, I opened my mind to activate my ability.

...can't believe she didn't tell him, Paul thought.

It was true then.

"You helped me qualify for the Nuclegene trials?" I asked.

"Yes. Listen, Logan, I'm sorry," he offered. "I hope you're not upset with your mother. She was just doing anything possible to try and help you. Any parent would've done the same."

I held up my hand.

"I'm not angry, just surprised," I said. "I love Mom. But now I realize I need to thank her for a lot more than I already have, that's all."

He adopted a sheepish expression.

"So, how did you manage to get me into the treatment program, exactly?" I asked.

He paused, as if gathering his thoughts.

...better to tell him everything, Paul thought.

"I'd just been selected as the Vice-Chairman of the House Science and Technology Committee," he said. "I wrote a letter to Nuclegene asking that you be seriously considered for the trials. They'd already closed the sample group, but I managed to have them add you onto the list. Hell, we'd already formed a subcommittee to investigate Nuclegene's proposal, and frankly, the science was impressive cutting edge stuff."

"Thanks for your help, Paul. I had no idea," I said.

I was stunned. It occurred to me that without Paul's help, I might already be dead.

"Glad to help out an old army buddy," he said. "Or rather, a good friend."

Next, I wondered just how much he knew about the results of my treatments.

"I feel almost like a new man now that the treatments are over," I baited.

He looked at me and his eyes narrowed slightly.

...more than that, I'd imagine, came his stray thought.

"I heard something about that, actually," he said. "How are you dealing with it?"

"You heard?" I asked.

He took in a deep breath and let it out slowly.

"You'd be surprised what I've heard and read about," he replied.

"So, did you also know from the beginning that the treatments might manifest these abilities in the patients?" I asked.

He shook his head and softly whistled.

"Now, there's a hot potato issue," he said. "No, I didn't. And if we had, my Congressional committee probably wouldn't have allowed the trials to take place. We approved a recommendation to petition the FDA to permit an experimental cancer treatment drug to go into immediate human trials, not an experiment to create super humans."

It made sense. Though for selfish reasons, I was suddenly pleased Nuclegene hadn't let that particular cat out of the bag ahead of time.

"Now look at us. Here we are," I said.

He sighed. "Yeah, here we are," he said.

"So, is this why you wanted to meet with me tonight?" I asked.

"Not entirely," he said. "Actually, I'm here to ask that you consider accepting Nuclegene's employment offer."

That was definitely unexpected.

"What? Why?"

"Logan, I'm going to shoot straight with you on this. And, believe me, that doesn't happen very often with politicians."

I couldn't help but feel amused over that.

"First, you've got to tell me how you knew about the job offer," I insisted. "Was that your idea, too?"

Paul appeared taken aback.

"No," he said. "Earlier today, I received a phone call from Nuclegene's president, Clive Bernard. He told me about the offer that he'd made to you."

"That bastard told me not to tell anybody," I groused.

"I'd say he's worried that you're not going to accept his offer," Paul said. "After all, he spoke to you more than a day ago. Geez, Bringer, most people would've accepted the offer before he made it out their front door."

Yeah, well, I wasn't most people.

"I'm just not sure I want to throw in with that lot," I said. "Yeah, they cured my cancer, but now I've learned they're conducting international espionage against some other shadow company over corporate secrets, and for all I know, agreements with other governments."

"Continuance Corporation," Paul said.

Once again, I was surprised.

"How in the hell did you know about Continuance?" I asked.

"Remember your meeting with Bob Tevin?" he asked.

"You know Tevin?"

"Deputy Director in NSA/CSS," he said. "Yeah, he briefed us on Continuance. And on *you*, I might add."

"*Us?*" I asked.

"Yeah, I'm also a member of the House Homeland Security Committee."

Wonderful. Paul sure gets around.

"For Pete's sake, do you sit on *every* committee on Capitol Hill?"

He laughed.

"Actually, that's the two that I'm particularly active in," he said. "And Tevin's one of the good people, so you can trust him."

I considered what he just said.

"Well, I liked Tevin on first impression, at least," I said. "Damn sure, he's a hell of a lot more likeable than *Special Agent* Prichard from the CIA."

Criswell chuckled.

"Prichard's a pain in the ass, even toward us congressmen. That ink pen episode Tevin told me about cracked me up," Paul said. "Bringer, you're a riot."

I didn't know what to say to that.

"Criswell, maybe you should tell me what you *don't* already know," I challenged with an edge to my voice.

My friend's expression turned serious once more.

"We don't know what Continuance is planning to do next," he said. "That's why it may be in your best interests to accept Nuclegene's job offer. They're in a position to leverage resources that the government can't touch...*legally*."

That brought an entirely new dimension to the topic.

"You mean *I* can do things that the government can't," I asked.

He pointed his finger at me.

"You got it, Bringer," he said. "Between all these competing intelligence agencies, they sometimes can't tell their asses from a hole in the ground."

Listening to him talk sounded just like old times. It was good to know he'd kept his down-to-earth sensibilities about him.

"Listen, I got into this to protect my family," I affirmed.

Criswell nodded. "You can still do that. Again, you can operate outside the system. But then, you can also leverage government resources through the FBI, as well."

Made sense, really. It might be the best of both worlds if what he said was correct.

"Do you trust Nuclegene?" I asked directly.

He appeared amused.

"You mean, *after* they misled a Congressional subcommittee and violated who knows how many federal statutes on improper experimental testing on humans?" Paul asked.

"Good point," I conceded.

Criswell reached out to clasp my shoulder with one hand, just like he used to do years ago.

"Logan, I can't order you what to do here," he said earnestly. "All that I can do is offer advice. And yes, I know you didn't ask for it in the first place."

I nodded. "Fair enough."

"However, your country could really use your help on this one, my friend," he said. "And I can assure you, you'll have friends who can help you through tight spots now and again."

"What kind of friends, Paul? Who are we talking about?" I asked.

He paused, as if considering what to say.

I opened my ability again.

. . . Conway and Brooks, among others, Paul thought.

"Powerful friends," he said.

"Republicans?" I asked, trying to get him to come clean.

He looked at me sharply. "Maybe. Who do you mean?"

Who told him? Criswell thought.

"Dammit, Paul, you're in bed with Republican Senator Benjamin Conway?" I demanded. "You're a democratic representative from New York, for Christ's sake."

Criswell shrugged sheepishly.

"Hey, I'm hardly in bed with the republicans. And I don't know who told you, but yeah, we collaborate on key pieces of legislation from time to time," he said. "Listen, I know that guy, Conway, is way over the top on most things."

"You mean, as in right-wing-extremist-whack-job kind of over the top, right?" I demanded. "As in, 'America might just get owned by corporations during my lifetime' over the top?"

He laughed. "Okay, Bringer, you make a good point. But I haven't drank the punch just yet, so calm down. There are some ideals I refuse to compromise on. Still, he and I agree that terrorism by international corporations isn't a good thing. And then there's my fellow Congresswoman Tonya Brooks from here in Iowa. She's a moderate republican at least, and she helps to balance things out with Conway. Between the three of us, we can pull together a powerful voting bloc. He's also a close personal friend of President Graydon, which could be useful from time to time."

I shook my head. "Man, you're way in over your head on the Hill, aren't you? It's no wonder you barely have time for a phone call, buddy," I mildly chastised.

"I did check in with your mom from time to time," he said.

Well, that was worth something.

"As a matter of fact, thanks for that," I offered. "It really meant a lot to her…and to me, too."

He looked back at me in a familiar, reassuring manner that I hadn't seen in years.

We both fell silent, and I sighed heavily.

"All right, Paul. I'll seriously consider Nuclegene's offer," I said.

"Good, and thanks," he said. "But hey, don't forget that you can always counter-propose things on your offer."

Counter-propose?

"I hadn't considered that," I admitted.

I'd never been very good at haggling. The process usually just pissed me off, resulting in me getting too annoyed to bother with it.

"Works for us politicians most of the time," he said.

"How would you like to help me out with that?" I asked.

He gave me a sardonic look.

"Yeah, right, Bringer," he retorted. "I could get into enough political trouble just for advising you on this issue. Let's think of this as a conversation between old friends and call it a night."

"You politicians are simply priceless," I said.

"Yeah, well, just keep my cell number handy in case some shit hits the fan," he said. "Of course, knowing you, Bringer, it'll be sometime soon."

I gave him a sour look.

"Very funny, mister comedian," I chided.

His eyes grew way too big for my preference, and he muttered, "What the---"

I heard a fizzling sound, and spun around just in time to see a rocket propelled grenade headed down range at us from across the dimly lit park.

Only barely managing to raise my shield between it and us, the projectile impacted my invisible barrier and ricocheted into the grand display next to us. The concussion from the explosion knocked us both to the ground as bits of marble, rock, and hot metal showered around us.

I felt partially stunned as my hearing still buzzed from the explosion. Flames licked at shrubs and grass near us, and I thought I heard muted gunfire. A bullet impacted the ground just an inch from my hand, casting a small plume of dirt into the air next to me.

My military training kicked into high gear, and I immediately reached for Criswell, who was still trying to push himself up from the ground.

I grabbed him by the belt and dragged him with me as I hauled us toward the still smoldering monstrosity of rock near us. Artistic value notwithstanding, it nevertheless seemed to be the most defensible structure near us.

"Just who the hell is firing at us?" Criswell demanded as he vainly tried peering around our impromptu cover.

"I dunno, but I think the shit just hit the fan," I said.

He glared back at me.

"Not funny, Bringer," he said.

I pressed my cell phone into his hand and urged, "Call 911. Then speed dial Megan Sanders. She's FBI."

"Me? Just what the hell are you planning to do?" he countered as two small bullets impacted the ground near my foot.

I sought the direction of the incoming rounds, trying to discern if it was the same shooter or a second one.

"Offense. Using the element of surprise."

He looked at me like I was insane.

"With *what*, exactly? Are you going to uproot a tree and throw it at him?"

"Trust me," I said. "And keep your damned head down!"

I manifested my shield, hoping it had the kind of coverage I'd need. As in the Nevada house fire, I tried to smooth out the shield into a larger area, all the while imagining a rigid shield like the Romans used in ancient times.

Then I stepped into a hailstorm of bullets coming from two angles.

Rounds impacted my barrier and ricocheted off in various directions. I rushed in the direction of the shooter to my left, the one with the most dangerous angle of fire at Paul.

A rapid succession of bullets impacted the front of my shield, causing small pangs of irritation inside my head. Thankfully, I sensed that I was bearing impacts much easier than on prior occasions.

I rushed forward, desperately concentrating on holding my shield in place while also trying to spot the assailant. I managed to spy a small muzzle flash of light to my right and barreled toward it.

Four bullet impacts later, I spotted a dark-haired man less than fifty feet away wearing black fatigues and leaning against a tree truck while holding a high-powered assault rifle.

I opened my right palm at my side, trying to create a fireball in my hand while also trying to maintain a shield. Fire sputtered in my hand and I sensed my shield fading as two rounds impacted the barrier.

Both bullets were suspended before me in the barrier while the flames in my hand extinguished. My head pounded from the strain I was enduring.

The whole situation made me angry, and I rushed toward the gunman at a dead run. All I wanted was to pummel the bastard with my bare fists.

I tried to focus on my shield again, and I practically felt it slip back into existence. Fortunately, I raised it back into place just in time to deflect two more rounds.

The resulting stabs of pain in my head suggested that the strain on my talents was increasing.

I could see the gunman's eyes widen as I drew closer to him, and I let out a roar of frustration as I charged him.

He let his rifle drop to the ground and drew a large-bladed combat knife as he slipped from behind the cover of the tree trunk. His eyes narrowed with the grim, steely determination of someone who intended to win.

But then, I felt much the same way.

Using the last bit of concentration for my shield, I forced it further ahead of me until it impacted the gunman. His blade momentarily deflected against it and his body was thrown backward a couple of feet.

It was just the edge I needed in order to catch him off balance as I slammed my fist into his jaw.

My training kicked in as he swiped his large blade toward me, and I caught his wrist with my left hand. I punched him in the eye and temple with two quick strikes, feeling pain shoot through my knuckles in the process.

Using the momentum of his counter-stab toward me, I neatly swung his arm into a natural arc, slamming the blade home into his abdomen.

The guy screamed in pain, and I used his distraction to punch him once in the throat and again to his temple with as much velocity as I could muster. He dropped to the ground unconscious, and I grabbed the assault rifle next to his body and stripped a full magazine of ammunition from his belt pouch.

Sirens wailed in the distance from multiple directions as I tried to raise my shield again just in case the other assailant was nearby. Desperate to return to Criswell, I ran through the park to where I'd left him.

I heard the telltale sound of another rocket propelled grenade launching off to my left. I spun toward it and the round bounced against my shield, exploding with full force as I was thrown to the ground.

I fell onto my back with an impact that nearly took the air from my lungs. The ground around me was on fire, including parts of a small tree next to me.

I drew a painful breath to refill my lungs; the scent of burned wood and leaves was also drawn in through my nostrils. I coughed once before staggering to my feet.

Adrenaline coursed through my body as I forced flames into my right hand and scanned the area for my next assailant.

I concentrated on spinning the flames into a tight fireball, fueling the effort with both anger and steely determination.

No more mister nice-guy.

I managed to catch a glimpse of movement ahead of me from the shadowy cover of some bushes. The figure was shouldering an RPG for another launch.

Throwing the sphere of fire from my hand, I propelled and guided it downrange from me toward the assailant.

His RPG fired, but the projectile veered off to my left, sailing past me in a matter of seconds. The resulting explosion occurred some distance behind me.

My fireball impacted the bushes next to the guy and fire erupted around him. He dove into a crouch, patting at his black fatigues as he ran.

Take that, asshole!

He ran to his left, and in the momentary light of the flames, I easily caught a glimpse of red hair.

It had to be our assassin from Chicago.

I started to pursue him but Criswell yelled off to my right.

"Bringer!"

I turned toward him, thankful he seemed no worse than when I'd left him. His wide-eyed expression suggested that he'd just seen my little fireball counterstrike.

"My God, Bringer! How the hell---" he shouted.

I tossed him the assault rifle and the full magazine, and ordered, "Shooter off to your right! Get the hell behind cover, and fire at *anybody* that looks threatening!"

He nodded once and turned around in a semi-crouched position, scanning the area ahead like he was taking point on patrol.

Like me, his dormant training must have finally clicked into action.

Criswell had been a damned good soldier.

As he went through the process of clearing his weapon and reloading, I frantically searched the tree line to my right for the assassin. There was no way I intended to let him get away again.

This business had to end here…tonight.

CHAPTER 19

Sirens blared all around the area as I scanned the park, running in the direction our assassin had headed. Despite the pounding in my head, I opened my mind to thoughts around me.

At first, there was nothing, then something faint entered into my mind.

…back to the car, came the frantic voice.

He was trying to get away.

I ran across the expansive park like a man possessed, frantically scanning for my target.

No longer the predator, he was now my prey.

I caught a quick glimpse of a dark-clad figure glancing back over his shoulder as he headed toward one of the park exits not far from me.

He spun toward me and fired two rounds from his pistol.

My shield went up and the two rounds suspended before me. I cast them back downrange at him but failed to see where the bullets impacted.

Running as fast as possible, I pursued him.

I was out onto the sidewalk outside of the park when I saw my target running toward a nearby sedan. The car's lights flickered on and off a couple of times, and the trunk lid popped open ahead of him.

As I ran toward him with my shield in place, my head pounded and throbbed. I had to be stretching the limits of my abilities.

The roar of an engine sounded behind me, and I looked back over my shoulder to see one of our city's police cars racing up the street in my direction.

I waved my arm at them and pointed toward the assassin's car ahead of me.

As I whipped my head around to focus on my target, I spotted the guy holding another one of those damned RPG launchers in his hands. It was pointed at me, but then he pivoted to his left and launched the round toward the oncoming police car.

I tried to extend my shield while shifting it to my right to deflect the round, but I was too slow and the maneuver too difficult.

The police car exploded behind me, and I turned just in time to see it careening in my direction.

Fortunately, my shield was in place enough that, rather than stopping the vehicle, my body was thrown in the opposite direction. The police car rammed into a nearby parked vehicle with a crashing sound of broken glass and crumpled metal.

I managed to flatten my body and roll as I'd been trained, but the hard asphalt still sent shudders through my body as I impacted it. I rolled to a stop along the opposite side of the street, narrowly managing to avoid slamming my head into the concrete curb.

My entire body coursed with pain, including the pounding inside my head, but I managed to force myself to my feet. My target had already shut the trunk and started his vehicle as I staggered back into the middle of the roadway.

His car sped forward up the street before I could try to conjure another fireball.

"Dammit!" I shouted.

He was getting away again.

As the sedan sped away, no less than three police cars nearly simultaneously appeared further ahead, blocking his progress.

Yes!

I started to run up the street toward the sedan, though to my body, it felt more like a painful canter, at best. The car's brake lights came on as the vehicle spun around in a semi-circle, its tires loudly squealing on pavement.

The sedan accelerated back down the street toward me at a rapidly increasing velocity.

Oh, shit.

With no immediate cover, I vainly ran to the side of the street, hoping to avoid getting hit. However, the sedan kept turning to keep me squarely in its sights.

I was about to become a hood ornament.

At the last second, I used every fiber in my body to propel a shield before me, even as I instinctively fell back onto the street. The weight of the vehicle pressed me onto my back, flat against the pavement.

The car launched into the air above me, as if impacting some invisible ramp. My head nearly exploded with pain as little stars appeared on the periphery of my vision. I watched the car's undercarriage as the vehicle rotated in a semi-circle above and over my head.

Seconds later, and somewhere behind me, the car impacted with a loud crashing sound. As I managed to roll onto my stomach, I saw the sedan lying at an angle against a parked vehicle; steam pouring out from beneath the hood.

I heard vehicles rushing in my direction from back up the street, as well as the wail of sirens.

As I pushed myself to my feet, my body was wracked with pain. I felt something running down my lip and onto my chin.

A quick swipe of my hand revealed fresh blood.

My blood.

Then I heard the driver's side door to the sedan pop open.

You've got to be kidding.

The bloody-faced assassin adopted a menacing scowl as he pulled himself from the wreckage, dragging another RPG-ready launcher from beside him.

I was barely able to stand as I forced fire into my right palm, desperately concentrating on spinning it into a tight ball. My head throbbed and pounded until my vision started to blur.

Tires squealed behind me, and I heard car doors opening, even as the RPG was being leveled at me.

"Logan!" yelled Agent Sanders.

Having run out of time, and likely energy, I flung the fireball from my right hand toward the car. The RPG fired, causing the projectile to whistle in my direction.

I closed my eyes at the last second as I threw my left hand up before me.

My head exploded with a mix of searing pain and mind-numbing shock as I felt myself falling backward. Intense heat raged around me as I felt fragments of superheated brick and mortar shower across my body and onto my face. My ears loudly buzzed from the sound of an explosion before me.

Seconds later, my body was being dragged across the asphalt, and I opened my eyes enough to see a burned body amidst the flames of the scorched sedan. To the left of where I'd fallen, a smoldering hole in the side of a building was the stark testimony to my shield's last-second success.

I looked up to see Sanders pulling at my right arm while a shocked-looking police officer tugged at my left.

"Hard asphalt," I managed to croak from my dry throat.

"Oh, please just shut up, Bringer," Sanders said as she stared down at me glassy-eyed.

* * *

Hours later, I lay atop a hospital bed, still wearing my smoke-tinged clothes. My scarred leather jacket was draped across a nearby visitor's chair, looking as if it'd just been through a war.

Battle-tested, I preferred to think of it.

Whatever the doctors had injected into me had finally helped my throbbing headache to ebb to manageable levels. An IV was still plugged into my left arm, restoring my body's fluids.

I took a deep breath, feeling some aching in my ribs from the effort. It was amazing how dehydrated a body could get from casting fireballs and dodging exploding RPG rounds.

God, how I hated RPGs.

Between those damned RPGs and the roadside bombs, they'd been every soldier's nightmare back in the Middle East.

The door to my room opened, and Maria peered in at me with a smile.

"Maria!" I greeted.

"Hey, hero," she said. "Feeling any better?"

"Yeah, actually. Whatever the doctors gave me helped a lot."

"Good. It was a concentrated solution I concocted just for you," she offered in a self-satisfied tone. "Kind of like your vitamin shot but with a kicker."

The woman's talents were being sorely wasted as a physician's assistant. I reached out to hold her hand as she stared down at me.

"Thanks, I appreciate that," I said.

Then Lexi and Kevin peered into my room, so I visited with them and Maria for a little while longer before closing my eyes and drifting off to sleep.

I felt so exhausted.

A few hours later, it was nearly midnight, and the doctor's reluctantly agreed to release me. They'd wanted to keep me overnight for observation, but all I really wanted was a hot shower and a soft bed.

Lexi and Kevin offered to take me home, but then, at the last minute, Agent Sanders showed up to insist on doing so.

As Sanders helped me with my tattered jacket, Lexi gave

me one of her knowing smiles, but I rolled my eyes at her and shook my head.

Don't go there, little sister.

On the ride home, Sanders filled me in on what had happened after I killed our renegade assassin.

"There wasn't much left for evidence once the firemen doused the flames," she said. "Still, I'm happy enough knowing he's finally dead."

At least we both agreed upon that.

"Oh, Congressman Criswell told me to thank you for what you did at the park tonight. He also said for you to 'remember everything he said to you'," she imparted. "He seemed particularly impressed with you, by the way."

I looked out the car window to the relatively benign world outside. My conversation with Paul suddenly seemed like a lifetime ago.

"We've seen a lot together over the years. We go back a long way," I said elusively.

"Some lives saved back and forth, I suspect," Sanders said.

"Yeah, something like that," I said.

"Hey, I bet the press is having a real field day with this," I added, partially to change the subject.

Sanders looked over at me with a wry expression before returning her attention to the road before us.

"What an understatement. We're crafting it somewhat differently as a failed attempt to assassinate a sitting congressman. Although the press is curious why Nevis Corners has suddenly become such a dangerous place since the Wallace Building explosion," she said. "Luckily for you, so far we've managed to keep your name out of the spotlight."

"And I couldn't be happier about that."

She winked at me.

"Hey, I've been thinking about tonight, and something keeps nagging at me. When I met Criswell in the park, he told me that only he and his administrative assistant knew about our meeting tonight. So, just how did those assassins find out about it? Because I sure as hell didn't tell anyone else."

She shrugged.

"Maybe they were already staking you out," she suggested. "Forensics is still collecting evidence but I'm hoping we receive some quality data to review relatively soon."

I looked over to see Sanders frowning as she drove.

"Of course, we also wondered how our shooter had known to show up in Chicago, as well," she said. "I'll inquire into the prospect of wire taps, as well as any prospective surveillance authorizations. You've already been followed by who-knows-what agency."

"There's been a possibility of an inside leak somewhere," I said.

"I'll run a check on Criswell's assistant, just as a precaution," she said.

I resigned myself with the realization that there were few secrets left in the world. Eventually, word gets out about everything.

But what bothered me in our case was how quickly it had happened.

* * *

I slept like the dead once I'd taken a shower and fallen into bed. It was nearly ten o'clock in the morning when the doorbell finally woke me up.

Sanders brought coffee with her when she stopped by to give me my vitamin injection. While she didn't seem to be in a hurry, I was too tired to bother asking her to show me how to inject the damned thing myself.

I thanked her for both the coffee and her time. Rather than making a snarky comment, she merely winked and patted me on the back before leaving to head back to the office.

"Next time, I wouldn't mind a hug," I teased as she

walked out my front door.

"Get over yourself, Bringer," she snapped as she stepped off my porch. "And please do your best to haul your lazy butt down to the office by one o'clock."

I just smiled, then took a swig of my coffee and watched her drive off.

Lexi called to check up on me, as well as Mom. I even chatted with Dad on the phone for a few minutes. He told me he was proud of me, which made me feel pretty good, given everything.

And I took some pride that, for the first time in weeks, I felt that my family was safer for my actions the previous evening.

Then my thoughts returned to the conversation I'd had with Paul Criswell. He'd made a number of good points, as well as revelations, concerning Nuclegene Corporation.

I felt a little better knowing that Continuance Corporation was making it onto a number of watch lists and government radars. With luck, maybe that would force the company to go further underground for a while; maybe even become inactive.

I wondered how an outfit like Continuance still managed to be referred to as a corporation. It hadn't been that many years since we were all worried about rogue nation states; now we sweated over rogue companies.

What the hell was the world coming to?

It took another hot shower and some ibuprofen before I managed to move around without considerable pain. My body had taken a lot of punishment in a relatively short period of time.

Still, I felt a sense of hopefulness for the future.

My future.

CHAPTER 20

By the time I made it into the downtown FBI office, it was straight-up one o'clock. However, I was amused from seeing Sanders look down at her watch while shaking her head slightly.

"Well, you're punctual, at least," she said.

"It's 1300 hours. Reporting for duty," I said with a wry expression. "Anything interesting to share?"

"Oh, you have no idea," she blandly replied and pointed to the desk nearest to her. "You can sit down at that computer and start typing a detailed account of what happened last night."

"Yeah, right. In case you hadn't noticed, I'm just a civilian," I said. "Shouldn't someone officially employed here be doing this?"

"You're a volunteer, remember?" she countered.

Busted.

I groaned, which, by the look of satisfaction on her face, provided her considerable amusement.

"Just great," I said. "Bureaucracy finally rears its ugly head."

Two hours later, I'd completed what I thought was a relatively thorough recounting of everything that had happened.

Sanders scanned the hardcopy version, and muttered, "Not bad, actually."

Then the two of us met agents Tara Collins and Ben Foster in the familiar conference room down the hallway from the main office.

I looked at Collins appraisingly, admiring her fitted knit slacks, which hugged her attractive hips and butt in all the right ways.

She smiled back at me with a glint in her soft blue eyes.

With no sense of guilt, I opened my mind to listen in on stray thoughts as I casually scanned the room.

…how much better that chest of his looks without that shirt, came Collins' thought.

Yep, I was definitely intrigued by Collins at some levels.

…gotta' finish that report before heading home tonight, came Foster's thought.

…making eyes at her like some slick player in a bar, came Sanders thought.

Sanders glowered at me when our eyes met, which jolted my concentration, and I immediately lost touch with the minds in the room.

"What?" Sanders suspiciously asked.

"Nothin'," I said with a shrug, deliberately looking past her to the wall of windows revealing the cityscape.

Moments later, Chuck Denton and Deputy Director Tevin walked into the room and took seats at the head of the table.

"It looks like I'd better set up an office here in Nevis Corners," Tevin quipped.

Agent Denton explained that Tevin was tasked to preside over the investigation into what was being touted as an assassination attempt against Congressman Criswell.

Then I was grilled by everyone in the room for details on the events, including recounting my story from scratch. Sanders asked clarifying questions to the report that I'd just typed for her, as well.

"Any idea who the assassins were?" I asked.

"His body was burned pretty badly, so forensics will need some time to work with the coroner's office," Foster said.

"And how did the guy know I was meeting with the congressman?" I asked. "Criswell said only he and his administrative assistant knew about it."

"Well, our burnt assassin had been following you and Sanders, as well as staking out your house," Denton pointed out. "Maybe the park was a location of opportunity?"

"And he brought a friend with him," I said. "Why not just take me out at my house, then? Why go to the trouble for a public location like the park?"

"We thought we had a leak early in the investigation," Sanders said. "Maybe there are additional leaks, including in Criswell's office."

"Yeah, but what would the motivation be to kill Criswell?" I countered. "To my knowledge, he hasn't had an active role in what's taken place."

"Collateral damage?" Agent Collins suggested.

"Perhaps. Still, it's an angle we'll want to look into further," Tevin noted.

"Agreed," said Denton.

Little else was brought to light that I thought was useful, and it took the remainder of the afternoon before the meeting ended.

As everyone rose from the table to leave, Tevin took Sanders and me aside.

"Bringer, your performance was pretty damned impressive last night. Aside from the proliferate damage to public property, and the unfortunate death of two local police officers, you still helped to keep the casualty count to a minimum," Tevin said. "Son, don't let this go to your head, but your value just tripled overnight. You're practically a hero now."

"I really wish that you hadn't emphasized that," Sanders groaned. "He's going to be insufferable now."

I flashed her a dirty look before shaking hands with

Tevin.

"Thank you, sir," I said. "But I wouldn't want a repeat of last night's events."

"Neither would I," Sanders quietly added.

I spared her a quick glance, but her facial expression was neutral and her eyes didn't meet mine.

"Are you feeling okay?" Tevin asked with concern.

"I'm serviceable," I replied.

"Good to hear. You stay serviceable," Tevin said, briefly clasping me on the shoulder. "We may be able to make good use of you again before this Continuance investigation is over."

"I'm making Continuance my personal project as long as they remain a threat to my family," I affirmed.

"Deputy Director, Bringer almost got killed last night. It would make things a lot nicer if the FBI could do more to *legitimize* his assistance," Sanders pointedly noted.

I appreciated her saying that, and I had to admit that I wouldn't mind an offer of financial assistance. Granted, I already had one, but it was from a company that I still had serious doubts about.

"That thought has crossed my mind," I agreed.

Tevin sighed and nodded.

"True, but I'm afraid I'm not in a position to do more than thank you at this time," he apologized. "However, I'll see what I can do. For the time being, please know that the bureau does genuinely appreciate your assistance, as well as putting your life on the line. You're a bona fide patriot, Bringer."

With that, Tevin left the room, leaving Sanders and I staring at each other.

"Bona fide patriot, my butt," Sanders scoffed. "More like free ride for the government, if you ask me. I mean, what agency *wouldn't* appreciate free telekinetic services for as long as it lasted?"

I nodded, thinking much the same thing myself. As much as I was in this primarily for personal reasons, the bureau was more than happy to leverage me to their advantage, as well. Their *unpaid* advantage.

Admittedly, and despite my reservations, Criswell's recommendation the previous night regarding accepting Clive Bernard's Nuclegene employment proposal sounded better with each passing minute.

But, did I want to get into bed with a huge corporation that had already treated me as a blind guinea pig?

I looked outside through one of the room's large picture windows, observing the waning sunset with a frown.

The swift passing of time surprised me. Had it nearly been a full day since I'd killed two assassins?

To be sure, I'd expected similar acts of violence while deployed in the conflict-plagued Middle East, but not in the middle of the United States. In Iowa, no less; arguably one of the safest, most boring places in the world.

"You okay, Bringer?" Sanders prompted with concern.

I stared into her hazel eyes and nodded.

"Yeah, sure," I said.

As we walked back to the main office, I asked, "Got any dinner plans tonight?"

"Bringer, please tell me you're not asking me out on a date," she challenged, though with a hint of amusement.

"What, are you kidding?" I countered, holding the door to the office open for her. "Hell, I'm just getting hungry and was hoping that the FBI might pick up the dinner tab."

"Keep hoping," she replied with a gleam in her eyes. "But I'm game for something, if you're interested."

"Oh, I'm definitely interested," I quipped, to which she looked at me with a surprised expression.

It satisfied me to no end to catch her off guard like that.

We barely made it through the door and into the office before a loud booming noise sounded and the building rumbled with a series of small reverberations.

Everyone in the room momentarily froze in place.

"What the hell was *that*?" Agent Collins demanded.

One of the office phones rang, followed closely by two

more. Agent Foster answered the one closest to him as Denton and Tevin appeared through the small doorway into Denton's office.

Then the building's fire alarm sounded.

The sound of an explosion came from outside, resulting in another shaking of the building. A plume of dark smoke rolled upward past the exterior windows.

"You're fuckin' kidding!" Foster demanded with an incredulous expression as his phone's handset was practically plastered to his ear.

A strange, high-pitched electronic alarm pierced the air in conjunction with the fire alarm.

"Our building's under attack!" Foster exclaimed as he slammed the handset back onto its base.

An FBI office building was under attack? The very idea seemed foreign to me.

"What? By whom?" Tevin demanded.

"Everybody, vests and heavy arms, now!" Denton ordered.

As everyone, including Sanders, scrambled toward a nearby line of reinforced cabinets, I rushed over to the windows to search below for what was taking place.

All I could see were people scrambling about as black smoke and flames poured from both the building and a couple of crumpled vehicles that were overturned. I also heard people screaming.

The door to the office slammed open.

"Hurry up, you guys!" called a security guard who'd already drawn his pistol.

Deputy Director Tevin and agents Denton, Foster, and Collins, all wearing vests and carrying heavy weapons, squeezed past the young man as he held the door open.

"What's going on downstairs?" I demanded as Sanders pressed a bulletproof vest into my hands.

The young rent-a-cop, who looked barely old enough to even own a gun, appeared wide-eyed with shock.

"S-some…guy…just threw a bus into our lobby!" he

stammered before running down the hallway to catch up with the agents.

CHAPTER 21

"Threw a bus?" I demanded while shrugging into my protective vest.

Sanders glared at me. "Hurry up, Bringer, we've gotta' get down there!"

She sped across the office toward the door with a shotgun cradled in her arms as I followed closely at her heels while buckling my vest into place.

My thoughts were jumbled as we blindly rushed down the hallway toward the nearby stairwell.

This is turning out to be another one of those days.

Then my mind settled into the mode I'd become accustomed to lately—the mindset of the combat zone.

You rarely knew exactly what you were stepping into; you just had to quickly assess your circumstances and react based upon your training.

Only, I didn't have any training for what I might be facing, though I tried not to think about that.

As we descended the stairs, I managed to take one deep breath just before Sanders and I barreled through the door and into the lobby.

We were greeted with a loud crashing sound from the front of the building followed by a small car sailing through the air toward us.

I grabbed Sanders by the arm and propelled us both to one side onto the tile floor. I formed my shield just as the hood of the car impacted the tile, casting shards of glass and other shrapnel around and against us.

"Find cover!" I shouted, then launched into a dead run through what had become a debris-strewn lobby.

Smoke filled the formerly stately-looking lobby as a small fire burned against a nearby wall. A large metropolitan bus lay on its side, and I heard shouts and screams from inside as fire-rescue attempted to extricate them.

Police, security guards, and civilians alike crouched in place behind furniture and decorative rock support columns, each person's face reflecting a mix of horror and disbelief.

"Get these people out of here!" I shouted, dodging mangled debris and obstructions as I headed to the lobby entrance.

Sporadic gunfire sounded, closely followed by the sounds of ricochets and muted impacts.

The building's entrance was a series of large, jagged rends and holes where vehicles had been cast either against the building or through the pane glass front façade.

"Our rounds are bouncing off!" a nearby police officer yelled into his radio as he crouched behind an upended patrol car.

Bouncing off?

Trucks and cars were overturned and burning, and black clouds of smoke billowed into the air around me.

Agents Foster and Collins simultaneously fired shotguns toward the main street as my eyes focused on their target.

A man of medium height and average build stared back at me with a sneer as bullets suspended before him in midair.

"Bringer," he said. "So, you finally came to play."

His broken English was accompanied by what sounded like an Eastern European accent.

Not that I was a linguistics major.

Then he chuckled, and projectiles quickly whistled downrange at me and against my shield, only to ricochet in other directions.

"Feel free to intervene anytime, Bringer!" Agent Denton shouted from behind the safety of a concrete barricade as he rammed a fresh magazine into his automatic rifle.

I realized I needed to shut the guy down, but based upon the carnage around me, I felt as if I was in way over my head.

"Who are you?" I demanded, stalling for time, as I tried to determine how best to handle the situation. "And how do you know me?"

His contorted facial expression gave him a sinister appearance.

"My name doesn't matter," he said with a glance over his shoulder at a nearby construction area. "And neither do you."

The guy never even moved as a cement mixer truck parked not far away flew into the air and barrel-rolled in my direction, sloshing mixed cement in all directions as people screamed or shouted around me struggling vainly to extricate themselves from the area.

I barely managed to fling my body out of the landing zone before the vehicle crashed against the building and crushed an upturned police car that I'd been standing next to.

Shards of pane glass mixed with a hail of building façade exploded behind me, showering the area with additional debris. An entire section of the second floor gaped open to the outside world.

More gunfire erupted around me from multiple directions as the sounds of approaching sirens filled the air. Agent Sanders appeared beside me, crouching behind a concrete barrier.

"Can you stop him?" she asked.

I didn't have a freaking clue.

"Get everybody outta' here, fast!" I shouted.

She nodded, but the look in her eyes told me that she wasn't feeling hopeful, either.

A number of additional police cars and a tactical vehicle stopped just down the street from the immediate war zone. As the newly arrived reinforcements confronted our miniature Godzilla, I moved further away from the building and around burning vehicles to get closer to my target.

I conjured a burning ball of flame in my palm.

His sharp look in my direction indicated that I'd hardly left his radar, and his eyes immediately focused on the fireball.

As fresh gunfire erupted from the tactical team, a nearby construction crane abruptly shifted from its secured position, arcing into the air toward the line of authorities. Bodies flew in all directions in a desperate attempt to avoid being crushed.

The crane flattened two patrol cruisers and nearly demolished the tactical team's vehicle.

I launched my fireball at him, but he deflected it to the street beside him as if he'd smacked aside a lit matchstick.

That was a bad sign; very bad.

A child's wails caught my attention and I looked to my left to see a young boy of no more than four fleeing from behind a nearby car for the safety of a bakery shop.

"Kyle!" screamed a woman who darted from behind a hiding place to pursue the child.

The rogue attacker barely cast a look in their direction before a power pole snapped in half, dropping toward them.

I extended my arms toward the woman and child, desperately trying to force my protective shielding in their direction. Yet, instead of blocking the impact of the pole, at least I managed to use my shield to push them out of harm's way.

The momentary distraction was nearly fatal for me as a sports car flew at me from my blind spot. In the last second before impact, my shield reformed before me.

My body was thrown twenty feet or more by the force of the vehicle's impact. Only my involuntary roll on the asphalt prevented me from being crushed as the car rolled over me to crash against the brick façade of the building behind me.

Shrapnel of brick shards and glass pelted my shield as I struggled to force air back into my lungs.

I was sorely pissed over feeling horribly unprepared and

ill-equipped to confront my opponent.

Additional gunfire momentarily erupted but was muted following subsequent crashing sounds and screams.

This has to stop now!

Ignoring the aching in my body, I regained my feet and formed a fireball in each hand while seeking my target.

"So, you are a fire man!" quipped our attacker.

A helicopter roared overhead, and a sniper took multiple shots at the man from the chopper's open side door.

The rounds harmlessly ricocheted away from him.

I launched both of my fireballs at him, to which he appeared momentarily surprised by the pair of them.

Nevertheless, he cast them aside; one erupting against a dump truck as the other one bounced across the asphalt to extinguish with a flash against a concrete curb.

A whistling sound pierced the air and I looked up to see a streak of smoke intercept the police helicopter. It burst into flames, plummeting in my direction.

Angling my shield upward, I retreated from beneath the chopper's impending crash zone. A man's flaming body hit the ground just before the helicopter made a metallic crunching sound against the pavement.

I maneuvered closer to the cockpit but quickly determined that both pilots were scorched and lifeless.

Gunfire erupted from remaining members of the tactical team at the roof of a building where the former smoke trail had originated from.

This guy has a fire support team?

"We're done playing now!" the man yelled in his clipped accent.

An invisible force punched against my shield, knocking me to the ground, and I felt as if my head had just been pummeled by a boxer's fist.

The man advanced toward me.

Another helicopter appeared overhead, and the guy barely spared a glance up at it. A second later, the chopper seemed to waver in midair as its engine groaned under some invisible strain.

I tried regaining my feet as I watched the helicopter change from hovering to falling. The man regarded me with a self-satisfied expression as the chopper careened toward me.

Once again, my shield formed as I hastily managed to stagger away from the crash zone at the last second.

The helicopter landed on its side with a metallic crunch as one side of its primary blade tore into the pavement and broke into dangerous fragments. The pieces shot in all directions, including many shards that impacted my own shield.

A nearby police officer was hit by debris, and he fell to the ground making desperate gurgling sounds.

My opponent shifted closer to the downed helicopter as yet another invisible force impacted my shield, knocking me to the ground.

I hastily envisioned an invisible sphere and cast it toward him, but he merely chuckled as it bounced against the helicopter, shifting the downed hulk slightly.

"Amateur," he chastised. "My time is wasted here."

My thoughts were awash with a bitter sense of futility when inspiration struck.

I sought a pile of iron rebar from the nearby street construction area, reaching out to them with my senses.

I desperately drew them back toward me, hoping to catch the backside of my opponent.

Unfortunately, his shield encircled him, and the rebar either bounced against him or impacted the chopper's metal underbelly.

That appeared to amuse him.

"You are like pitiful child," he teased.

A series of gunshots sounded and I saw the rounds halt before the man's face. He sneered and instantly cast them back in the opposite direction.

A series of muted grunts and shrieks sounded from behind me; the sounds of further suffering.

I was out of ideas.

I'm not strong enough.

"Our visit is done here." The man concluded. "Too bad."

I was also out of time.

The smell of jet fuel assailed my nose as the man raised his arms for the first time, pointing them in my direction. Despite my shield, I felt my breath being slowly squeezed from my body.

My head pounded from the strain of maintaining my shield as I tried to breathe while nearly choking on nearby fumes.

Fumes!

My eyes focused upon the wet pavement beside the helicopter as fuel trickled from the chopper's fuselage where metal rebar had pierced it.

I sneered at the man, who frowned at me in a puzzled fashion.

Igniting a fireball, I jerked my arm forward, casting it to the ground.

"No!" The man said with sudden realization.

The air beneath him ignited in a blaze of flames, catching his clothes on fire as he flailed around and screamed.

A single, intact rotor blade remaining on the nearest downed chopper caught my eye, and I reached up to grasp at it with my talent.

Gritting my teeth from the pain that shot through my brain, I jerked my arm down. The length of mangled rotor blade snapped off, arcing downward to sever the flaming man's upper body in half.

His smoldering body fell to the flaming pavement in two pieces as I staggered away from him with my shield reformed.

The chopper exploded, and the concussive force slammed me to the pavement. My ears rang and buzzed as I vainly struggled to retain consciousness.

Agent Sanders appeared at my side and helped me up. Together, we staggered away from the burning carnage.

"Are you okay?" she demanded with a wide-eyed

expression.

I only managed to nod, coughing while inhaling air back into my lungs.

A rapid series of gunshots came from the direction of the building where I'd seen the earlier smoke trail, and I turned in time to see a lone body falling from the roof to the pavement below as tactical team members rushed toward the building.

"We're clear!" someone yelled. "Move in!"

The area was suddenly assailed by firemen, policemen, paramedics, and ambulance technicians as the wounded or worse, were attended to. A showering mist of water was blowing in multiple directions from numerous fire hoses as Sanders and I moved toward the center of the street and out of the way.

I couldn't help but notice that a number of people were casting wary looks in my direction, some reverent and some not.

A non-descript black helicopter appeared overhead, practically hovering atop us, and I looked up at it to see a sniper in the open doorway shouldering a rifle.

Instinctively, I generated a fireball in each hand and moved away from Sanders.

"What?" she demanded.

I stared up at the helicopter, trying to determine its intentions as it hovered directly overhead.

"Logan, I think it's one of ours!" Sanders yelled.

"I don't care! Get it the hell outta' here!" I shouted.

A nearby tactical team member spoke into a handheld radio and the chopper quickly veered away.

I maintained my fireballs in each fist while scanning the immediate area around us, including nearby rooftops. It appeared that friendly tactical team members had already taken up positions there.

Chuck Denton stopped not far away to stare at me, warily regarding me as if I were something dangerous and unpredictable.

I slowly turned in a circle in the middle of the street, seeking my next target; wondering who or what might be coming next.

"Logan! We're okay now," Sanders tried to reassure me.

I took a deep breath and allowed the two fireballs to dissipate from my hands. Wisps of flames fell harmlessly to the asphalt beside me.

"No," I said. "We're far from okay right now."

I took in the disaster zone around me, watching black smoke billow into the air from multiple burning fires and seeing emergency responders vie for control of the situation. The cries of wounded and the shouts of barking orders from emergency personnel filled the air.

I felt partially shell-shocked as my mind fought to take it all in at once. It was sensory overload, not to mention my head was pounding like there was no tomorrow.

Then a stark realization dawned upon me.

I'm not the only one; I'm not unique. And even worse, I'm not even very accomplished at whatever I am.

My ass had very nearly been handed to me that day, and I wondered who else might be out there waiting to come looking for me.

Something dark and certain in my mind told me there had to be others.

But who the hell were these people?

More to the point, I wondered how on Earth I'd successfully manage to confront them.

ABOUT THE AUTHOR

Jaz Primo is a history aficionado, "pun-master", and all-around fan of vampires. He authors paranormal romance, urban fantasy, and young adult literature, and has enjoyed a fulfilling background and career in higher education, including teaching U.S. History classes during evenings. Jaz lives in the Great American Midwest with his wife and a long-lived cat.

You can find Jaz Primo online at the following locations:

Website: http://jazprimo.com

Facebook: Jaz Primo

Twitter: @jazprimo

Sunrise at Sunset
Sunset Vampire Series, Book 1
by Jaz Primo

When is a bloodthirsty predator the best protection against a psychotic killer? When the predator is both a vampire...and the woman you love.

"We vampires are focused and tend to shape our own realities."
My name is Katrina Rawlings, and I am a vampire. I declare that with neither pride nor ego. I am simply nature's most dangerous predator. On occasion, it's a very valuable quality. It helped me protect Caleb Taylor one day when he was very young. But that single, traumatic day is behind him now; wiped from his memory, or so I hope.
Caleb has finally matured into a rather striking young man, and believe me, I like what I see. I'll readily admit that there are issues for us to confront and overcome, though a sense of mutual commitment isn't one of them. I'm feeling hopeful for our future together, in fact. But an adversary from my past has returned to haunt me, and she's trying to get back at me through Caleb. That was her first...and last...mistake. I'll protect my Caleb at all costs, and I'll make her regret the day she was born.
So, I suppose that I'm not just a vampire. I'm about to become someone's worst nightmare!

Available in trade paperback and all major eBook formats!

Go to http://jazprimo.com/books for purchasing links!

Winner of the Paranormal Romance
Guild's Reviewer's Choice Award for
Best Young Adult Novel of 2012!

Gwen Reaper
A Young Adult Paranormal Romance
by Jaz Primo

Boy meets beautiful and mysterious, yet reclusive, girl who harbors a potentially-lethal secret.

"A thing of beauty is a joy forever: its loveliness increases; it will never pass into nothingness." John Keats, English romantic poet.
I never thought that my first exposure to real beauty would be tinged with the threat of oblivion…

~ ~ ~ ~ ~

When high school junior Scott Blackstone is forced to move from his childhood home in Springfield, Illinois to small-town Custer, South Dakota, he expects nothing less than to languish in complete disappointment. Instead, he discovers a beautiful and mysterious seventeen-year-old girl named Gwen, who captivates him from his initial, adrenaline-laced sight of her on the shores of Stockade Lake. Scott's pursuit of the elusive Gwen sweeps him into the midst of a potentially lethal family heritage that was birthed in hope, only to be passed into a legacy of guilt and death.

Scott engages in a journey of discovery, tinged with both angst and danger. Like many dire legends throughout history, he is unprepared for the untimely revelation that both love and despair are often two sides of the same coin.

Gwen Reaper
(A Young Adult Paranormal Romance)
is available in trade paperback and all major
eBook formats!

Go to http://jazprimo.com/books for purchasing links!

A Bloody London Sunset
Sunset Vampire Series, Book 2
by Jaz Primo

In *A Bloody London Sunset*, a timid spirit rises to assert himself, a forbidden love sparks, and a forgotten past threatens to topple the power of love.

Katrina Rawlings is a vampire who has finally rediscovered happiness for the first time in centuries. But unwanted complications erupt with a vengeance. Decisions of necessity combined with dark memories from a forgotten past threaten her relationship with the love of her life. When a sacrifice must be made, can she endure her decision?
Caleb Taylor's life is finally back on track. He has rebounded from a near mortal injury, both physically and emotionally. Yet, his reality is shaken by the suggestion of a betrayal of trust from the woman he loves. Can the power of love overcome the power of a lie?
Paige Turner is a century old vampire who fearlessly revels in a simple existence pursuing blood, dancing, and sex. Simple needs, and all met in the same manner: hot, fast, and without regrets. But a spontaneous visit leads to heartfelt sacrifice, and unexpected complications strike fear to the core of her soul. Will she survive the revelations?
In the exciting second novel in the Sunset Vampire Series, a trust is betrayed, bonds of friendship are strained, relationships may end, and a tenuous neutrality among the world's vampire population is threatened. With stakes so high, some will not survive A Bloody London Sunset!

Go to http://jazprimo.com/books for purchasing links!

Summit at Sunset
Sunset Vampire Series, Book 3
by Jaz Primo

Does the fate of one innocent human soul outweigh the needs of the entire vampire race?
The third, and most exciting, novel in the *Sunset Vampire Series* has finally arrived!

Powerful vampire Katrina Rawlings and her human mate, Caleb Taylor, are once more drawn into dangerous circumstances. Representatives of the most powerful and influential vampires from around the world converge upon a scenic mountain retreat located in Slovenia's Upper Bohinj Valley for a summit of historic proportion. Mystery leads to treachery, and events quickly spiral out of control. With the fates of both vampires and humans in jeopardy, Katrina desperately struggles to reconcile the balance of worldwide vampire power against honoring her commitment to the love of her life. Unwilling to be rendered helpless, Caleb initiates a desperate gamble that leads to a mortal decision. Meanwhile, the sexy and sassy vampire, Paige Turner, spearheads her own mission involving both surprising revelations of heart and grave circumstances for those around her.

In *Summit at Sunset*, unlikely alliances will be sought, eternal bonds of friendship will be tested, unrequited love will be unleashed, blood will be shed, and one pivotal person's fate will collide with destiny.

Available in trade paperback and all major eBook formats!

Go to http://jazprimo.com/books for purchasing links!